FOUND

POWERTOOLS: THE SHIELDS, BOOK 1

JAYNE RYLON

HAPPY ENDINGS PUBLISHING

V2

eBook ISBN: 978-1-947093-23-2

Print ISBN: 978-1-947093-24-9

Cover Design by Jayne Rylon

Editing by Mackenzie Walton

Proofreading by Fedora Chen

Formatting by Jayne Rylon

ABOUT THE BOOK

From New York Times and USA Today bestselling author Jayne Rylon comes a steamy new multi-partner standalone series set in the Powertools universe.

The Shields security team accepts missions in the grey area of both law and morality that no one else wants or can handle. They're a ragtag bunch of special ops soldiers, ex-government agents, and hackers wrangled by a former construction worker who aspired to be a superhero's sidekick when he grew up.

What could go wrong when they turn their sights on a human trafficking ring that might have been the reason their coordinator's sister disappeared nearly thirty years ago?

Nolan Skalbeck is sure their assignment is a bad bet. Regardless of whether or not they find the hauntingly gorgeous woman their artist sketched or not, the horrific things he discovers about the operation they've infiltrated convinces him they have to shut it down for good by whatever means necessary.

What he doesn't expect is to fall for a woman who

already has a partner, and is willing to share him with Nolan. Once he has, it will take every bit of his strength and training to keep from losing them both.

Even if he's successful, how will he convince them, himself included, that he's not a horrible person—like the ones they've been surrounded by for most of their lives—even though he hunts and destroys evil bastards for a living?

ADDITIONAL INFORMATION

Sign up for the Naughty News for contests, release updates, news, appearance information, sneak peek excerpts, reading-themed apparel deals, and more. www. jaynerylon.com/newsletter

Shop for autographed books, reading-themed apparel, goodies, and more www.jaynerylon.com/shop

A complete list of Jayne's books can be found at www. jaynerylon.com/books

1

_____

Adrenaline spiked in Nolan's system. He took a deep breath and then another as he slipped through the forest under the cover of a moonless winter night. Careful to exhale in a slow, thin stream, he avoided making a puff of frozen mist anyone lurking nearby might spot. The barely audible snap of an occasional twig from his left was the only hint that Sola was doing the same, not too far away. The woman was stealthy as fuck.

"That's it. Everyone steady. Careful now." Jordan, their boss, sounded as if they were going for a stroll in the park instead of crawling through enemy territory.

The earpiece Nolan wore was his lifeline to the outside, to a place where everything was safe and bright and sane. His tenuous connection to a world he hoped to return to if he didn't get himself killed during this mission. At least until the next time he had to descend into some special hell. After all, this was his job. Kicking ass and making things right. Fighting for people who weren't able to do it for themselves. The goals of the "security" team he worked for, the Shields, were always aligned with due north on his moral compass, even if the methods they used to eliminate targets weren't always entirely legal.

Nolan deepened his crouch, aware that not even his obsidian cargo pants and turtleneck made of a heat-signature dimming material would be enough to obscure his bulky form if one of the soldiers who worked for the sex trafficking ring they were about to invade got curious and looked a little too closely in their direction.

"I'm in place. Have a visual on the primary target." Aarav, their sniper, clocked in precisely on time. The man was practically a robot. Unflappable, which encouraged Nolan to try to rile him incessantly while they were hanging out at headquarters. Of course, the only person who really had a chance at ruffling him, and probably not even she could while they were engaged in business, was Sola, though she didn't seem to realize it. Behind the scope of his rifle, Aarav was a machine, and when it came to looking after Sola's fine ass, he'd be twice as diligent, even for him.

"The trackers show Sola and Nolan approaching from the south, right on course." James, their newest addition —a completely adorable former construction worker who'd always aspired to be a superhero's sidekick— coordinated their efforts from the Shields' headquarters. He hadn't much enjoyed his single foray into fieldwork a couple months ago, but the guy was a legend when it came to keeping them in line from the office.

Doubly so tonight. Considering how important this particular assignment was to him, James was on top of his game. His voice was calm and matter-of-fact in Nolan's ear, helping to keep him focused. He said, "JRad is standing by to cut the power. Scheduled for 253 seconds from now. Let me know if anyone needs more time."

"I'm good," Aarav answered for all of them. Nolan and Sola would only break radio silence if something was wrong. Same went for Ransom and Levi, who were mirroring their approach from the other side of the better-days building that used to be some sort of canning facility in the way back. It had been converted into a seedy hideout where women—and apparently underage men as well—were bought, sold, and used.

Nolan thought again of the particular victim they were attempting to find a trace of. Laurel, James's long-lost sister. They'd gotten a tip that she'd been kept in this hellhole once, though he figured that was a pretty way of saying tortured. Unfortunately, it had been years since any of their leads—who'd been freed with the Shields' help after a similar raid they'd done not too long ago—had seen her. Someone here would know something to carry them up the next step in the chain. They were closing in on answers, he could feel it. And until they had them, he'd be happy to put an end to the sick bastards who continued to abuse those who couldn't fend for themselves.

Nolan desperately hoped, for James's sake, that they got some closure. He'd be lying if he said his own curiosity wasn't piqued too. Questions had been clawing at him from the moment he'd seen the artist's renderings of what Laurel could look like today. Maybe it was because he had a very beautiful face to put with the unspeakable crimes. Or possibly, knowing she was James's sister made her easier to relate to than some of the other victims they'd rescued. Either way, her portrait had struck such a chord with him. He hadn't been able to get those haunted eyes out of his mind for months.

"I've got the entrance locked down." Marcus had reached his post at the main gate. He'd keep anyone from coming in to provide backup or slipping away from the justice they were about to deliver. Kennedy, their medic, was with him. Far enough from the main action to be protected, but nearby so she could get to the operatives in the thick of things in a hurry in case things went sideways. Marcus seemed nearly as rabid about watching her ass during ops as Aarav was about Sola.

When Nolan reached the edge of the clearing, he glanced over at her. She flashed him a hand signal for ready, which he echoed. Their body cams sent the data to James, who rallied the team. "Ransom, Levi, Sola, and Nolan are all in place. Aarav is set. Marcus and Kennedy are on standby. JRad is on final countdown. Twenty-nine, twenty-eight, twenty-seven..."

Jordan came over the intercom next, giving orders that set their intricate plan in motion. It took months of planning but came down to moments of action if they did their jobs right. They were a precision instrument working together in what was about to become a cloud of chaos. The next several heartbeats could change Nolan's life forever.

Silence from their objectionless teammates was as good as a green light. James gave them one last boost. "Good luck, everyone."

JRad, an honorary Shield, a geek-turned-Dom who worked for an elite police squad called the Men in Blue and did...well, *this*...with them as a side hustle on occasion, gave the final count. "Three...two...one."

Everything went black.

The forest erupted into motion and violence, dragging Nolan into its inky depths. He sucked in a lungful of air as if preparing to freedive, then entered the mix with Sola, who set the pace for their spear of the overall attack. Music cut off from inside the building and time appeared to distort, going slow and fast all at once.

His comms picked up a few dull thuds that he recognized as silenced shots.

"The exterior guards are down except for one runner who was grazed. Marcus, he's heading straight your way. Sola, Nolan, Ransom, and Levi have crossed the clearing and are about to enter through the ground-floor windows." James gave a play by play so they were all up to date and didn't accidentally take out one of their own as they made split-second, life-and-death decisions.

Aarav grunted. "Inside they're slow but moving, herding most of the victims toward the basement, except for those *occupied* upstairs."

If Nolan's boot bashed through the window a bit harder than necessary, he figured no one would notice or care. His blood boiled as he tucked and rolled, popping up with his weapon drawn. It didn't take long before he'd eliminated three of the fuckwads hurting the young women he saw scurrying toward safety behind couches. He wondered how often they'd faced violence that they had learned to huddle together and keep low as they sought shelter.

That thought alone made it easy to pull the trigger when he needed to. Beside him, Sola was doing her part just as fluidly until there was no one left to take out in the vicinity.

He swept through the main area, then flipped around to face it as Sola began to climb up to the second floor. As they moved back to back up the stairs, a shot took a chunk out of the wall beside his shoulder. Oops, guess there was someone left down there after all.

Nolan could have sworn he felt a breeze on his neck right before the head of the guy pointing his gun at him exploded like a ripe watermelon. Damage most likely due to a large caliber shell. "Thanks, Aarav."

"You're welcome." They both knew if that asshole had felled Nolan, Sola would have been next.

Unfazed, she jetted down the hallway, kicking in doors, and using zip ties to restrain the monsters they found inside each room while Nolan covered her and took out a few more of the dudes who tried to stop them with bullets instead of those who could only cower seeing as they were equipped with bare asses. Those guys they tied up and piled in one room for someone else to sort out later. If the patrons thought they'd been engaging in independent, consensual sex work, well, that wasn't something they took issue with. But anyone who saw these women and, fuck it, kids should realize that wasn't what was going on here.

The Shields coordinated seamlessly, like one single righteous weapon. And before things had barely begun, they were over.

"Our section is clear. That's everyone cleaned from the top floor," Sola reported.

"Us too," Levi confirmed. "The basement is now varmint-free."

"Same at the front. No one in. No one out." Marcus wasn't usually a man of many words but on ops, even less so.

"The cellar door is still barred from the outside. No one else made it past the indoors crew," Aarav reported.

With the immediate threat eliminated, and Marcus's

eyes on the access road to make sure no reinforcements showed up, their attention turned toward the more important part of their mission. Making sure the victims were safe and well taken care of.

Ransom called for the medic. "Kennedy, we could use you in here. Brace yourself. I wish I could kill these fuckers again."

Nolan hung back, letting Sola approach the freaked out survivors in their area. "Hey, you're okay now. We're not going to hurt you. We want to help you. Get you somewhere safe. Where you'll never have to do *this* again. Assuming you don't want to. And certainly never under these conditions."

She waved toward the dirty mattress in one of the rooms. He discreetly scanned every woman, man, and child, angling his chest so that he fed their images back to the Shields' headquarters for their records.

None of them were the woman he was looking for.

Now that the critical moments had passed, James's voice was a lot less sure and somewhat vulnerable when he asked, "Does anyone see my sister?"

"Negative," Ransom replied.

"Not me." Aarav sounded like he hated to confirm it.

Sola called Laurel's name as she checked a clump of women who'd hid in a bathroom. When she emerged, she shook her head. Nolan cursed then tapped his comms, hating to deliver the crushing blow to his friend. "I'm sorry, James. Laurel isn't here."

A whoosh of air was followed by several long seconds of silence.

"Okay. I guess that's good, right? Besides, we knew it was a long shot." James couldn't quite disguise the disappointment in his voice.

"Don't give up." Jordan, the owner of Shield Security Services and their undisputed leader, probably had settled his hand on James's shoulder at their command post in the mountain mansion Jordan lived in with his husband and wife, which used to serve as their temporary headquarters. Now that they were growing, James had taken on one final construction project overseeing the erection of a multi-story building that would include planning space, an armory, a gym, and adjoined apartments for their agents in Middletown. It would probably be less plush but way more convenient in the long run. Besides, they were more like family than co-workers, and staying together would only cement the bonds that helped them excel under intense conditions like these. "None of us will stop, James. Not until we find her or information about what happened to her at least."

Nolan grimaced. He knew what Jordan was really saying. They wouldn't give up until they'd found Laurel or discovered where someone had hid her body—and put them in the ground for it.

He thought again of the artist's rendering of the woman Laurel would likely be today—high cheekbones, melancholy yet proud eyes, and a strong chin that erased any misplaced sense of her delicacy. He'd long ago learned to trust his gut in this business. And his instincts were screaming that Laurel wasn't as far away as James might think.

They just had to keep searching and helping as many other people like her in the process.

"You're looking for Laurel?" asked a pale woman, older than most, wrapped in a stained blanket. "Wavy brown hair, about this tall, same age as me?"

"Yeah." Nolan tried not to act too interested lest he

spook her. "Her family is hoping she's safe. They love her very much and want to know she's okay."

"If that's true, what's her baby brother's name?" The woman stood a bit straighter, defiant despite her circumstances.

James gasped on the other side of the comms.

Nolan grinned thinking of James as baby anything. He was cute as hell but a full-grown man. "James. His name is James."

The woman blinked and a single tear rolled down her cheek. "I haven't seen Laurel in close to ten years. But last I knew, she was working at Heels outside of town, earning her way out from under Draven. No one ever makes it. She knew that, but she said she had to try."

"The strip club?" Not that Nolan had ever been to that particular establishment, but their briefing for the op had included it since it was part of Draven's network and one where shady shit happened.

"Yeah. Once the women here age out..." She shuddered. "Anyway, if they're pretty enough and haven't been broken, sometimes they *graduate* to the club. Draven says he'll give them a job so they can pay off their debt to him and go free. He skims most off the top. Charges them for costumes, makeup, a place to stay, food, all that. It's a waste of time and most either end up here again or...give up. I don't know what happened to Laurel. But she never came back. I knew she wouldn't, one way or another."

"We can work with that. That's great information. Thank you." Nolan's arms ached to hug their informant, but he was afraid she wouldn't derive any comfort from the touch of a stranger, so he simply nodded instead. "If you go with Sola, she'll make sure you're safe, have clean clothes, warm food, and transition you to our friends from a shelter that's equipped to set you up for success in whatever it is you want to do next. This nightmare is over for tonight and forever. No buyouts. No bullshit. Okay?"

"Who are you?" the woman asked, more tears streaming down her face. "Who would just...let us go? Help us? After all this time?"

"We're the Shields." Nolan smiled at her, nodded, then pivoted on his heel, not wanting to waste a moment. Once Draven got word of what they'd done here, who knew what he'd do next to protect what was left of his empire?

"Boss, I'm going to check out that club." Nolan hated the thought of returning empty handed, seeing James— who'd come to be a friend in addition to a co-worker over the past few months—heartbroken, even if he had a sexy husband and wife to console him properly.

"Now? On your own?" Sola raised a brow at him.

"These women will trust you a hell of a lot more than me. And a single guy will draw less attention at Heels." Nolan shrugged. "Kennedy is going to have the bulk of the work now. Help her convince these people to go to the safe house James arranged until Tom's organization can bridge the gap. Aarav will be happy to fill in as your partner in case you need someone to step and fetch. Won't you, buddy?"

"I'll be down in two minutes." Aarav had probably already meticulously cleaned and packed his weapon, which he babied.

"See?" Nolan grinned. "I'll catch up."

"You always get the fun jobs," Sola mock-bitched, but didn't try to stop him. Around Shields, everyone could hold their own, even in sticky situations.

"Going to a strip club is your idea of a good time?" Nolan couldn't help a little teasing of his own. "Maybe you should take Aarav out for a lap dance later to loosen him up."

"Don't involve me," the sniper deadpanned. "I could shoot you a new asshole from here."

Wow, something other than strictly business from Aarav. That's how Nolan knew that despite his feigned indifference, Aarav wasn't exactly impartial when it came to Sola.

She rolled her eyes, then refocused on the job at hand —ushering the victims of the shit-sacs they'd just ended to a sanctuary where they could recover then, once they were ready, move on with the rest of their lives. One of Jordan's mega-rich benefactors, Archer something or other, had bankrolled Tom's shelter, ensuring they had the resources they needed to help these people start fresh and hopefully, someday, be happy.

Like James, Nolan and the rest of the Shields wanted so badly for Laurel to have the same opportunity, even if she had no idea they existed. He hoped they weren't years too late.

2

Laurel stepped out of the shower and reached for a towel. It wasn't plush by any standard, but it was spotlessly clean. She breathed deep of the steam scented with whatever grocery store shampoo had been on sale last, happy to have scrubbed away the stench of grease and another too-long shift at the restaurant. She was getting too damn old for these marathon nights at work, but when Jace had a chance to stay longer and play another set for the decent crowd that had gathered to listen to his music, she hadn't been about to deny him his moments of glory.

Certainly not after all he did for her. He was her rock. The only thing she had in life she could count on, besides bills.

Laurel peeked into their adjoining bedroom. Her roommate was stretched out on the only bed in their tiny apartment. His tattooed shoulders rested on the wall as he reclined with one arm flung over and behind his head. The pose left his ripped abs on prominent display while he watched the news on TV. She licked her lips, though she knew tonight, like every other night they'd shared a bed throughout the years, he wouldn't dare touch her. Because neither of them were sure that she wouldn't freak out if he did.

Even that small mental reminder of what they'd lived through riled the ghosts from the deep, dark places they resided in her mind.

She braced her hands on the lip of the sink and hung her head for a few moments until the flashbacks passed, then looked up into the cracked mirror above it. Dark circles ringed her eyes and pissed her off. Laurel glared at herself. She'd never been one to wallow and wasn't about to let negativity bring her down now. Not when she had a pretty normal life, one she controlled, and enjoyed, when she wasn't so damn tired.

Laurel finished drying off, then brushed her hair and teeth before striding into the other room naked. She could feel Jace's stare on her ass and the curve of her back as she took her neatly folded pajamas from the dresser they'd scored off the curb one lucky garbage day. It was cute now that they'd given it a makeover, painting it and scuffing it strategically so it looked fashionably distressed instead of merely shabby.

Sort of like them.

She glanced over her shoulder and busted Jace. Not because she minded, but because she thought, maybe one of these days, he might admit that he wanted her as badly as she wanted him.

Hey, less likely things had happened in her life. Like escaping the evil bastards who'd stolen her from her family and abused both her and Jace for years until they'd managed to work their way free. They'd been told by Draven they could leave if they earned enough to pay off what he'd "so generously spent on their shelter and food" throughout the years. It had been total bullshit. They'd already made him a truckload of money when they were young enough to appeal to his sick clientele, but Laurel and Jace had stuck together, stripping and bouncing for the ring's club front, Heels, until they'd more than met Draven's requirements.

Of course that's when he'd tried to renege on their agreement. Somehow, mostly with the giant chef's knife stolen from the club's kitchen, Jace had convinced the man to let them go once and for all. It had been damn near ten years and thinking about it still gave her goose bumps.

To distract herself from bad memories, Laurel finished tugging on her pajamas, then wiggled her finger in front of the terrarium Jace had cobbled together out of salvaged window panes and screens. It had been her birthday gift two years ago, and sat in a place of honor on top of the dresser. Their lizard, Dottie Long-Tongue, trotted right over and greeted Laurel with a wag of her pretty yellow tail.

"Oh yeah, you need a bedtime snack, huh?" Laurel dropped in a few peas she'd snagged from the scrap pile at work. She chuckled as Dottie gobbled them up before scampering away into her favorite corner beneath a gnarled piece of wood to rest.

"I feel you, girl." Laurel sighed and sank into bed, leaving a narrow strip of mattress between her and Jace. Exhausted and on edge, she had trouble settling in.

"Cold?" Jace asked, frowning, as he noticed the tiny bumps lingering on her arms.

It was easier to say yes than to admit where her thoughts had gone—even for a moment—and have to reassure him that she was holding it together, so she nodded. Jace took the arm he'd been pillowing his head on and wrapped it around her instead, drawing her to his side.

Laurel snuggled up to him, resting her face on his chest. He stroked her hair as he stared straight ahead at the news. Neither of them commented when he drew the covers up to their waists, which she was sure had more to do with the bulge in his shorts than a non-existent chill. Not that it would have stood a chance against the furnace of his ripped body anyway.

It was torture to be so close to him and yet to be so screwed up, both of them, that they couldn't take what they truly needed from each other. It stung that he didn't think she was strong enough for him, or maybe that he didn't like the idea of having someone so many others had taken first.

Then again, Jace was no saint.

She didn't know the gory details, didn't want to, but there was no way to hide that he was a hookup pro or that he prowled club alleyways when he didn't think she'd notice him gone for a few hours. How could she not when they were so close, and when he acted so damn guilty every time he caved in and satisfied his needs?

Maybe someday she'd find the balls to ask him why he only fucked guys when she could damn well tell he was also attracted to women, including her. No wonder she was wiped out.

Laurel's mind raced nearly every moment of the day, trying to figure out how to survive this bizarre life she'd been tossed into while staying, mostly, sane.

"Thanks for working late tonight." Jace winced. "I should have cut things off earlier."

"Nah. You were enjoying yourself and you sounded so good. I was happy I got to hear more." She smiled up at him. They had little enough to be excited about—she'd never deny him his music.

"Seemed a shame to stop playing. Rudy was raking it in at the bar, and my tip jar overflowed."

"It was a good haul. Especially once people were a few drinks in. Always worked that way at Heels, too." Why did she keep thinking about that shithole tonight? It had been a long time since they'd been stuck there. She should be over it by now.

Jace squeezed her. "I think we might have enough put away soon that you could sign up for that social work course you were looking at."

He said it casually, but the way he stopped breathing made her sure he was afraid of how she'd react to that suggestion. And he was right to be nervous. Just the thought of reaching for a goal that big scared the shit out of her. As long as she kept her expectations low, she couldn't be disappointed, and that...

Well, a college course was a step toward enrolling in a degree program, a dream that could break her if she reached for it and flopped. It had been hard enough when they'd challenged each other to get their GEDs. Even basic things like that came with hurdles other people didn't face, like having to buy fake social security numbers from Draven to get state issued IDs so they could register to take the test since he refused to let them do anything to draw the attention of cold case cops to them...and then to Draven and his illegal activities by association. That move had allowed them to look for better jobs, both because they could say they'd finished high school and because they didn't have to rely on those willing to pay under the table anymore. Bit by bit, they'd dug out of the hole they'd been in. It had been hard, but they'd done it together like the team they'd been for so long now.

On her own...

"I don't know." She bit her lip. "It's probably better to build up our savings some more instead."

"For what, Laurel?" He frowned down at her. "We're good. We've already got three months of expenses squirreled away, and we don't splurge on dumb shit."

"I know, but we don't have health insurance. What if one of us gets sick? Can't work for a while? Or maybe we could pay for a few therapy sessions instead. God knows we could use a shrink ourselves."

Maybe if they did, they could work out the issues holding them back from a real relationship, one that could fulfill them both.

"If you need to go to the doctor, I'll pick up another job." He rolled toward her, rubbing her arm slowly and gently. She didn't fail to notice that he never thought of himself. If he got sick, he'd suffer in silence. And as for counseling, he could use it every bit as much as she could.

"You already have two, working at the pub and gigging at night." She shook her head. "I don't know. It seems unfair to blow that on myself."

"Well, when you snag that fancy career I'll freeload off of you. Deal?" He smirked, and she couldn't help but laugh since he wasn't the sort of man to ever ride someone else's coattails.

Laurel should have let it go, but some of her earlier thoughts wormed their way to the forefront of her mind. "We could use it as a down payment on a bigger place. So you don't have to share a room with me until you're eighty."

He jerked as if she'd kneed him in the balls, then disentangled himself, leaning away and making her afraid he might get up entirely. "Is that what you want? Privacy? I can sleep on the couch. I've told you that a million times."

"Exactly my point." She stiffened but put her fingers on his clenched forearm to soften her words. "Maybe *you're* the one who wants some personal space."

He slumped into his usual place and mumbled, "I'm good."

Then they were both quiet as they stared at the TV, pretending to watch the news when really they were avoiding the awkward silence that settled over them like a lead blanket. Laurel concentrated on Jace's heartbeat, counting the steady *thud-thuds* until she was half asleep.

So she almost didn't catch the breaking story that cut in on the late-night weather forecast.

Jace's reaction roused her, drawing her attention. He tensed beneath her, his muscles immediately ready to pounce, or flee, or fight like he'd done so many times before.

"What?" She bolted upright. Her gaze flew to the doorway, which was still empty and quiet. Habit.

Then she swung her attention to the TV. Red and blue lights painted over a building she would never forget. Just seeing the old canning factory made her dinner churn in her guts. It was the seediest arm of Draven's operation. The one where he kept his "bargain" offerings. It had been her destiny once, a place she thought she'd die before she and Jace had cut their deal and finally broken free.

"...an anonymous tip led police to the scene where we're being told multiple bodies, all male, either naked or heavily armed, were removed from the compound."

"Someone shut them down!" Laurel got to her knees,

wanting to run, to dance, to shout, but frozen at the same time.

"Holy shit. After all this time." Jace shook his head. "I wonder, why now?"

It's wasn't like the police hadn't known what was happening out there. Whether it was the fine print of laws that checked their power or good old-fashioned corruption that had prevented them from intervening, she had no idea, but this was damn near a miracle.

"Jace, what happened to the workers? There's no mention of the women and girls. The boys." She clutched his hand and he held on tight.

"I don't know. Maybe for their own protection?"

She wanted to believe that, but the system had let her down so many times she couldn't do it without proof. "I need to find out. What if this is their chance to run?"

"What are you going to do?" Jace stood then, as if he might block her from leaving if he didn't like her answer.

Fuck that. No one told her where she could and could not go these days. She arched a brow at him. It wasn't often she reminded him that she was six years older than him, but this was one of those occasions where she'd leverage any authority she had.

"I'm going to Heels. I'm going to find Cherri and get the scoop. If we can help even one person get away while things are disrupted, we *have* to."

"Absolutely not." He made the mistake of crossing his arms and spreading his feet.

"You don't own me." Laurel might as well have smacked him.

Jace staggered backward, then flung his hands up. "Fine. Go ahead. Put yourself in a position to be dragged into that pile of bullshit again. But I'm not doing it."

"I would never ask you to." Laurel tore off her pajamas, grabbed underwear and a pair of black jeans and a matching T-shirt, getting dressed in seconds flat. She snatched her purse off the dresser, shot one look over her shoulder at Jace, then bolted from their apartment. Jogging down the stairs, she hoped she could find a taxi to hail at this time of night.

3

Son of a bitch!

Why couldn't Jace ever get things right when it came to Laurel? He was always tiptoeing around some issue or another until he ended up tripping and blowing everything between them to hell anyway.

He pinched the bridge of his nose before reaching for his ripped jeans and the faded rock band T-shirt he'd stripped off at the end of what had already been a really fucking long day.

It took him a few seconds to stomp his feet into the scuffed black boots that were one of his prized possessions. Laurel had found them at a secondhand shop and given them to him for Christmas a couple years back, before they were as stable as they were starting to be now.

But if she ran off to Heels and got embroiled in Draven's world again, if she got hurt or worse, none of that would matter. Everything they'd worked so hard for would be for nothing. *Motherfucker.* He had to find her and either convince her there had to be a better way or—fuck his life—go in with her.

She was a hell of a lot braver than him. Always had been. The thought of coming within a mile of that place or anything to do with their old life made him want to puke. Someday, they were going to save up enough to get out of there, move to one of the coasts where no one would ever be able to track them down, and forget this dump ever existed.

They had to be alive to make it that far.

Jace bolted from their apartment and took the stairs to the street four at a time. He'd apologize to the little old lady who lived below them for making such a racket the next time he brought her groceries. He cursed when he saw the deep brunette of Laurel's still-damp hair vanish into a cab halfway down the block.

"Hey, wait! Laurel!" He waved his arms as he shouted, but she wasn't stupid or about to give him the chance to talk her out of trying to save the fucking world.

He jammed his hands in his pockets and watched his breath puff out in a series of tiny clouds highlighted by the flickering neon light of the pawn shop nearby as he panted, realizing Laurel had been right. It wasn't that he didn't want to rescue anyone else who might have scored a chance to sneak away from the endless nightmare they lived while part of Draven's empire. It was simply that he was a coward. Scared. For her. For them.

Doubly so now that she was doing this solo.

Jace jogged in the same direction Laurel had disappeared, toward the main crossroad, and prayed he could find another ride. It took a few precious minutes, but eventually he flagged down a cab and jumped inside. "Heels. Five bucks extra if you make it fast."

"Going to miss your favorite dancer, huh?" The man gave him a gross, knowing head tilt. "Or maybe something better? I've heard you can buy a lot more than a lap dance out there."

"Drive, asshole." Jace resisted the urge to punch something, preferably the cabbie's smug mug. He wished he'd been able to talk Laurel into spending some of their savings on cell phones so he could reach her while they were in transit. At least then he could have promised her that he had her back and that he'd never let her put herself in harm's way without him to watch out for her.

It seemed like it took three hours instead of five minutes to reach the club on the seedy fringes of the city, admittedly not too far from their neighborhood. They'd done the best they could for themselves and they were only going up from there...if they could keep flying under Draven's radar.

Truth was they were too old and too jaded to be of much use to the bastard anymore. But that didn't mean he couldn't turn their lives into a living hell if he chose to make an example of them. Or, for that matter, end them so they wouldn't do anything stupid, like trying to get him in trouble.

The cab hadn't even fully rolled to a stop when Jace tossed a ten into the front seat and hauled ass, tugging the hood of his charcoal sweatshirt up and slouching his shoulders as he tried to fade into the night. He didn't run for the light streaming from the front door, where bouncers stood on either side. No way.

It had been years, but that didn't mean someone wouldn't ID him.

Instead, he stuck to the shadows and edged toward the rear entrance where Draven imported women, not-so-grown girls, and young men from his various facilities at the start of each night and collected them after they'd served their purpose. Apparently, Laurel had the same idea. He spotted her right before she rounded the back corner of the building and whisper-shouted in her direction.

"Psst! Hey!" He didn't dare use her name.

But she didn't hear him. Nor did she notice the figure trailing her, moving like a panther through the jungle at night. Silent, deadly, and definitely stalking its prey. Oh hell no!

Jace's guts twisted as he watched the man pounce and ensnare Laurel in his arms. She thrashed, skimming the assailant's shin with her heel, but he was so much bigger than her, and so damn strong. He clamped his hand over her mouth, preventing her from screaming as he dragged her—not into the back rooms of Heels, thank God, but into the patchy woods next to it instead.

Jace sprinted for the spot where they'd disappeared. He wasn't even trying to be subtle when he crashed through the scrubby shit at the fringe of the trees and barreled in their direction. No fucking way was someone going to take Laurel from him. Not now. Not ever.

He loved her. Even if they never said the words or acted on the emotions underlying everything they did together, he knew she felt the same about him.

So when he saw that ginormous dude with oddly perfect hair—no flabby Heels bouncer either, but someone who knew his way around a gym—manhandling Laurel, Jace lost it.

The bastard was talking but Jace didn't pause to hear what he was saying. "Hey, calm down. Not going to hurt—"

Jace slammed into the bastard and didn't hesitate before plowing his fist into the man's super-solid ribs. He hoped he hadn't bitten off more ass than he could kick. This guy was fit as fuck and young. Seasoned too. He didn't seem fazed by Jace's attack. Until Laurel helped out by kneeing the dude in the nuts. Hard.

"Oof." He crumpled into the dirt, grabbing his junk. It looked like he was about to make some half-assed excuse that Jace was not about to give him the chance to utter. He popped the guy under his jaw and roared internally as his bright blue eyes rolled back in his head. Out cold.

"Shit!" Laurel glanced around frantically as she scrambled to her feet and flew to Jace's side. "You were right. This is too dangerous. Hell, it could even be a trap. I'm an idiot. Let's get out of here."

"We can't leave this guy here. The last thing we need is for him to run his mouth to Draven. He knew who you were, didn't he?" Jace scanned the area around them, but no other goons seemed to be approaching.

"Yeah. He called me by my name." Laurel groaned and nudged the bastard with the toe of her shoe. "What the fuck are we going to do with him?"

Jace didn't say anything. She must have read his mind, as she often did, because she waved her hands in front of her chest. "No. No way. We are not taking him with us."

"*You* were the one who was right, Laurel." Jace hugged her tight, trying to subdue her trembling, which he knew had no more to do with being cold than her goose bumps had earlier. "We've gotta help the people who were in the old canning station tonight, wherever they are now. This guy knows what's up with that. I'm sure of it. We'll get the info and then dump him. Come on, help me get him to the cabs."

"We're going to take him where? To our place? Do we really want him knowing where we live?" Laurel asked pretty valid questions. It wasn't like Jace took hostages every day, though. He wasn't an expert. What the hell option did they have? They had nowhere else to go.

"We'll blindfold him before he comes to and after we get answers we'll toss him in another cab back here or maybe drive him to a bus stop on the other side of the city." Jace sounded more confident than he felt.

"Uh..." Laurel didn't seem convinced, but she too seemed to regret the way they'd parted earlier. It was always like this with them. They were on the same path. They just couldn't get their shit together enough to walk in step. She licked her lips, making him wish for the thousandth time that day alone that he had the right to kiss them. "Okay. Fine. Let's do it quick before he wakes up."

Jace nodded. "He's a big motherfucker. Why couldn't he have been scrawny? Let's get our arms around him. Act like he's blackout drunk and I'll do the rest, okay? I'll hit his head on the window if he starts to come to."

"Yeah. Sure. Let's go." Laurel planted her feet and crouched before slinging one of the guy's arms around her shoulders. Several tattoos of much better quality than Jace's poked out from beneath his fancy jacket. The dude could probably hike to the North Pole without freezing to death in that thing. He didn't seem like one of Draven's regular henchmen.

Please, God, don't let this be another huge mistake. Jace cursed. When would their past leave them the hell alone? When would they really be free of it? Ever?

He used his anger to fuel himself as he levered the unconscious guy to something approaching vertical, his head lolling from side to side. Laurel steadied him on the other side, and together they waddled their way to where only one taxi was idling in the parking lot. Someone was ahead of them in line, but Jace said, with his best friendly grin, "Would you mind? I'd like to get this dumbass home before he gets sick again."

"Ah... yeah. Go right ahead." The dude waved them ahead and even held the door for them. No one wanted to be around for that.

"Thanks."

"We've all had those nights." The club patron chuckled.

Except they hadn't. Jace didn't drink to excess. Never had, never would, because the last thing he ever wanted was to be out of control of his situation again. No fucking thanks.

Jace leaned forward to tell the cabbie their address rather than shouting it—just in case—but when he checked on their captive, there was no hint the guy would be waking up any time soon. He hoped he hadn't seriously injured the fucker. He didn't want that on his conscience.

It was a shame he'd had to put his fist to such a pretty face. And that hair, damn. Even after their tussle it looked like it belonged on a Hollywood action movie star more than an everyday man.

Ugh. Jace must be hard up if he was thinking the evil prick who'd tried to steal Laurel was hot as hell. But he'd sure never seen one of Draven's stooges look like this before.

Laurel was peeking over Jace's shoulder too.

"You recognize him?" Jace murmured in her ear.

She shook her head, then stared out the window. It seemed like she might have been holding her breath until they pulled up outside their building. Then she came around to the curb and helped Jace wrangle the dude out of the car. Their captive groaned when Jace planted his shoulder in the guy's flat-as-fuck abdomen and hefted him over his shoulder, but stayed draped there as Jace hauled him up the stairs and inside.

It only took a minute before they'd sacrificed the tie from Laurel's robe and the cords from the toaster and a lamp to lash the bastard to one of their mismatched kitchen chairs. Then they stood back, getting their first good look at the man.

He seemed more like someone Jace would screw than one of Draven's lackeys. Black cargo pants doing a piss poor job of hiding shredded quads and his pristine windbreaker unable to camouflage his excellent upper body conditioning. What the hell had they gotten themselves into?

Jace went into the bedroom and grabbed a bandana, which he used to blindfold their captive.

Then he turned to Laurel. "What now?"

4

———

"**Y**ou're asking me?" Laurel's semi-shriek roused Nolan from unconsciousness. He stifled a groan when the pounding in his jaw and the base of his neck brought him the rest of the way out of his fog. He gingerly ran his tongue over his teeth to make sure they were all still there and not-so wiggly without alerting Laurel and the guy who'd come to her rescue that he was awake. "This was your idea!"

"I had to do something! You're the one who ran off without a plan and didn't even bother to wait a damn second for me to come around when you leapt out of bed and decided to singlehandedly save the world."

"Fuck. I didn't help anyone." Laurel sounded defeated. "The only thing I did was risk what we've built. I'm sorry, Jace."

Jace, huh? So that was the guy with the steely eyes who'd seen too damn much and knew his way around a street fight. He hadn't been suave, but he sure as hell had been effective and brave, attacking without hesitation. Nolan could appreciate that.

"Nah, it's me who fucked up. I should have stuck with you, no matter what. But I'm not as decent as you. I'm not a superhero. I'm just some guy who's trying to put his life together after being shit on. And, I admit it, the thought of being sucked back into that scares the piss out of me."

Now that made Nolan groan under his breath. The raw emotion, their vulnerability, and how easy it was for them to be honest about it with each other. Damn. These two had been through so much.

He probably shouldn't have touched Laurel, and certainly not in the aggressive way he had, grabbing her and subduing her as he hauled her into the woods. Except she'd been so damn close to giving herself away, and he was at heart a covert operator. Storming the club by himself, unprepared, to bring her out again wasn't a possibility. Losing her wasn't an option. No way was he going to report back to the Shields, and especially James, that she'd slipped through his fingers. He hadn't had time for subtlety.

It was only because Nolan had been trying to avoid hurting either of them that Laurel's bodyguard, boyfriend—or whatever the hell Jace was to her—had gotten that hook in. The one that had given her the opening to squash his poor balls, which even now felt like they'd been relocated somewhere around his navel. *Ugh.*

Still, it was obvious his captors weren't professionals. And he was.

Even now, he was sure the Shields were dispatching someone to his location. He, and the rest of their team, wore trackers for a damn good reason, and he hadn't reported a new intended destination. James would be on that deviation from the plan as quick as if his husband

and wife had invited him to skinny dip in the indoor pool at their temporary headquarters again.

While he appreciated the backup, it was obvious Laurel and Jace weren't a real danger to him. Probably.

It would take a hell of a lot of fast talking to convince them he wasn't going to harm them either. In fact, he thought he might be able to help them. If they'd let him.

"Excuse me. This is a really lovely moment you're sharing, but I thought you should know I'm eavesdropping." Nolan figured he might as well out himself. Then maybe they'd start to trust him. Of course, he'd sound more like a gentleman than a scoundrel if his voice weren't raspy as fuck after his impromptu nap.

"Son of a bitch!" Jace snarled, and Nolan scrunched his eyes closed behind the blindfold, half expecting to get walloped again.

"Who are you?" Laurel asked.

"My name is Nolan Skalbeck. I'm thirty-four. A Gemini. And I like snuggles on the couch while watching movies. What else would you like to know?" Why? *Why* had he said that? Especially when he couldn't read their expressions to see if his attempt at levity was having any impact at all. The Shields were always telling him his mouth and bad jokes were going to get him in trouble one day. He hoped it wasn't this one.

"Why were you stalking this woman?" Jace obviously had his head on straight despite being a novice interrogator. He didn't give away her name, though Nolan already knew it.

"I wasn't." Nolan hedged. "I mean, not exactly. I *was* looking for her, but not for any nefarious purpose, and I wouldn't have manhandled her like that if she hadn't been about to run into Draven's escalated security, who might not have believed her if she told them she was a free woman after tonight's drama. You know what I mean?" He drew a deep breath as he heard Laurel gasp. "If you let me go, I can explain everything."

He had to break their perception of him as the enemy. As their prisoner.

"How stupid do you think we are?" Jace sneered.

"I mean, I don't have any inherent objections to being tied up by a woman and man as hot as you two." Nolan grinned, trying to keep things light and disarm them with a flash of his straight, white teeth. "But you might as well take this blindfold off me. I'm not going to forget what you look like any time soon. I already know you're Laurel. And Jace, your big strong fella here, has straight dark hair, a handsome face, and the kind of build that comes from doing real work. He's also got some pretty identifiable tattoos on his hands and the side of his neck. While I didn't get a great look at them, I am wearing a body cam so the team at our headquarters definitely did. P.S. Feel free to wave hello if you like."

Okay, so that part was a fib. He *was* wearing a body cam, but it wasn't running at the moment.

"How do you know my name?" Laurel asked.

Jace hissed, "Don't tell him anything. He's probably guessing. Bullshitting us."

Nolan took a deep breath. This time it might be best to stick to the truth. These two obviously had trust issues, and for good reason. If they caught him in the teensiest lie, this game would be over. "I work for a private security service. We work on cases that land in the gray areas of the law, or where legal agencies can't quite cut through enough red tape to be effective. Basically, we stop trash human beings from hurting more people. Tonight it was us that took out the cannery. We shut down that arm of Draven's operation, because no one should ever be treated like that. But even more, we were really hoping to find someone in particular. You, Laurel."

"Why?" She whispered.

"Because your brother desperately wants to know what happened to you."

The sound of a dull thud and the vibration of the floor through Nolan's boots worried him. Despite his concern, he took the chance to shift in his chair and make some adjustments to his bonds. Meanwhile he asked Jace, "Is she okay?"

"Shut your fucking mouth until we ask you questions," he snapped at Nolan. Possessive enough that he was probably her lover. Yet he was so gentle it tugged at Nolan's heart when he murmured to Laurel, "I'll knock him out again right now. We can get in another cab and drive him somewhere far away, and you'll never have to deal with this if you don't want to."

Ah, now that was his kind of romantic.

"But what if I do?" Laurel's voice cracked. For a moment there was near silence interrupted only by the swish of fabric, making Nolan sure Jace was rocking her as he consoled her. His fingers clenched on the arms of the chair as he wished he could do the same.

Maybe for both her *and* Jace.

This was why he worked for the Shields in the first place. To make a difference in the lives of people like them who'd fallen through the cracks of an imperfect system. Victims who fell prey to assholes with enough money to corrupt. Dickheads with power they didn't deserve. He preferred to work on missions like these, where they were in time to improve the situation. Though if they weren't, he had no problem delivering justice instead.

Nolan held perfectly still when light, tentative steps approached. He didn't dare breathe to keep from spooking Laurel.

Her fingers were deft yet gentle as they slid the blindfold from his eyes and even paused to fix his hair, combing the front highlighted bits into their trademark swoosh before running them down the shorter sections at his temple as he so often did. He blinked into the buttery light of a miniscule, worn and dated, but spotless kitchen. "Thank you."

It said a lot about her, and how much better she was than the people who'd wrecked her childhood. Nolan fought the urge to lean forward and show his appreciation with a quick peck on the cheek. He didn't want to add a black eye from Jace to his already throbbing face.

"How do I know you're telling the truth? Maybe I don't even have a brother, huh?" She talked tough, but he could see the longing in her eyes, and he wanted nothing more than to give her what solace he could. Since he figured drawing her into his lap and attempting to mollify her by banding his arms around her in a protective hug would only result in her boot in his crotch...again...he stuck to his original strategy.

"James would be very hurt to hear you say that." Nolan winced, thankful he didn't have his comms engaged at the moment. He hadn't expected Laurel to trot past him the moment he'd arrived at Heels. No excuses, though. He was certain when he got back to the office Jordan was going to tear him a new one for not adhering to protocol and doing it before he'd stepped on site. That guy was not the sort of boss you wanted unhappy with your job performance either.

Laurel's jaw dropped open. Her gaze winged to Jace, who nodded slowly before saying, "Let's hear him out."

Nolan figured he was going to have to work extra hard since both of them rightfully questioned everything and didn't trust worth a damn. At least when it came to confronting strangers, it seemed like their bond was plenty strong. Must be nice.

For the millionth time since Nolan had met Laurel's brother, he wondered what it would be like to be in the sort of relationship the guy had with his husband and wife. Or one like Jordan had with his spouses— unwavering, fully committed, and hella hot. Nolan had been low-key obsessed with Laurel from the moment he'd seen the drawing of her, and watching her with Jace now wasn't dampening any of his curiosity. Something about them pulled him to the edge of his seat. Of course, these were the two last people in the world that he should be letting pique his interest. He knew enough about their history to realize that his purpose was to shelter them, not to mack on them.

Nolan reined in his inner horndog even if, for some reason, they made it harder than any other victims he'd ever interacted with.

He'd made a terrible first impression, practically mauled an abuse survivor, and didn't doubt for one second that they had some sort of intense yet dysfunctional relationship going already. The looks they shared were full of love, and angst, and far more drama than he preferred from the people he hung with. And yet...

He wished he could forget all this bullshit and help

them hash out whatever was off between them. Huh. He shook his head and returned his concentration to his mission.

"Yeah, you should. I mean, if I was planning to hurt you or scam you or some shit, would I still be sitting here shooting the shit with you even though I untied myself from this chair like five minutes ago?" Nolan shrugged, then slowly, very slowly, brought his open hands around to rest in his lap.

Jace's eyes went wide and Laurel took a step back. Jace angled himself so that he was between Nolan and Laurel.

They were so cute thinking they could detain him. Or keep him as their prisoner.

Well, shit, they were smoking, period, now that he got a good look at them side by side. Laurel he'd known would be a stunner from the moment he'd spied the artist's age-up of her. But her roomie—because the pictures of them magneted to the fridge proclaimed this was their joint apartment—could melt the snow that had started falling outside with just one look. He was defiant, rough around the edges, and obviously a loyal companion even if he made shitastic decisions.

For effect, and because his balls still ached, Nolan settled one ankle on the opposite knee. They really needed to work on their knot tying skills if they were going to truss up their guests in the future. He'd love to show them how sometime, if they were ever up for it.

"So you're what? Some kind of private investigator? Or a super spy or something?" Jace asked, making Nolan grin.

"That sounds a lot cooler than what I actually do for the Shields." Probably he shouldn't mention how efficiently they took out targets or that they were kind of into vigilante justice. "Her brother, though, he's legendary.

Made our whole office his bitch in a matter of weeks. Everyone loves James. And he misses you. Is worried about you, Laurel. I could call him for you so you can talk to him directly."

Laurel's lower lip wobbled for a moment before she drew herself up tall again. "I wouldn't recognize the sound of his voice today. It's probably different than when he was eight. If you really know James, then I'm sure you're aware I haven't spoken to him in decades."

"Well, quiz me then. I know him decently well." Nolan hoped he was up to the challenge. He thought back on the late nights they'd spent in the office while prepping for operations or the times he'd chilled with James, his spouses, and the rest of the Powertools crew off the clock.

Laurel tapped her chin for a second, then smiled. "Who was his favorite comic book character?"

"Easy. Still his idol. Robin." Nolan's grin spread slowly as he thought about the stories James had told and how he compared his work with the Shields to his childhood aspirations.

"Robin? Come on. That's the best you can do?" Jace huffed. "No one would pick him."

"James would." Laurel's eyes grew misty and Nolan wasn't sure he was going to be able to keep his hands to himself if she started to cry. He tucked them under his thighs, flat on the cracked seat of the chair as Jace gathered her into his arms and stroked her hair while never once taking his stare from Nolan over her head.

"You believe this guy?" Jace wondered.

"I do. Am I dumb?" Laurel obviously struggled with cynicism and wariness, which made perfect sense. What else could Nolan do to prove it to her?

"You're not," Nolan insisted, his tone a little rougher

than usual. "James also told me he used to do your hair and how he put that ponytail with the baby-blue ribbon and white polka dots in it for school picture day. It was the image they circulated when you disappeared. He told us your mom would leave you alone when she worked a second job at night and how you protected him from your uncle, even if he didn't realize that's what was happening at the time."

Laurel clutched Jace and sobbed. She sagged, but he was there to brace her and prop her up. He glared at Nolan even as panic flashed in his gorgeous brown eyes shot through with gold flecks. "She never cries. If you're fucking with her, I will kill you."

"I wouldn't blame you if you tried." Nolan kicked back in the chair, balancing on the two rear legs until it creaked ominously and he set it down carefully lest he break one of their few furnishings. "But you won't have to because I'm not screwing around. If you'll let me reach into my jacket, I can get James on videochat, and when you're comfortable, I'd like to take you somewhere safe. Somewhere you can meet him and verify for yourself that what I'm saying is absolutely true."

Laurel froze. "Oh. I don't know. What if...."

She looked up at Jace and he brushed the hair from her face. "You have nothing to be ashamed of."

She slammed her eyes closed but, after a few seconds, nodded.

"Do you have a gun in that coat somewhere?" Jace asked.

"Nah, it's in a holster under my shirt, near the small of my back. And there's a second strapped to my calf. You should have checked that as soon as you had me tied up."

Jace's eyes went wide.

"Not because I'm going to do anything with them." Nolan held his hands up. "But because it's what you do when you take someone captive."

"Jesus," Jace muttered. "I don't plan on doing this ever again."

Nolan chuckled. "Come and get them."

Jace nodded curtly, then stepped closer. Laurel took a frying pan from a hanging rack nearby and cocked her arm just in case Nolan so much as breathed wrong. He liked her style. Nolan gritted his teeth as Jace ran his hand beneath the hem of his T-shirt then along his abs, around his side, and into the small of his back. He hoped both Laurel and Jace were too shell-shocked to notice his cock twitching in his pants. He struggled to get his body to understand this was for business, not for fun.

Before Jace's explorations had hardly begun, he withdrew as if singed, the gun in hand. Then he crouched to retrieve Nolan's spare weapon too. Of course, he had a knife and a few other goodies left on him, but Jace had only asked about guns and they didn't have all night.

It wouldn't be long before the Shields raided this apartment if Nolan didn't check in and he didn't want anyone breaking what tentative truce he'd managed to negotiate.

"Okay, go ahead," Jace said as he stepped back, aiming the gun at Nolan. Thankfully the safety was still on and Jace's finger was a mile from the trigger, but still...

Nolan nodded and withdrew his phone from his pocket. He speed dialed their command center and put it on speakerphone.

"What the hell did you get yourself into?" Jordan asked immediately. It would be obvious since he wasn't using his comms that other people were likely listening in. So the boss was careful not to give too much away.

"Laurel's apartment. Want to say hi?"

James broke in, talking a million miles an hour, without much more training than his sister or Jace. "Seriously? You're not fucking with me right now, are you? That would be an awful joke, even for you, Good Hair."

Laurel snorted at the nickname, and Nolan frowned, resetting his do into its place. Hey, no one could blame him if it was a little unkempt after the night he'd had so far. "See for yourself."

Nolan tapped the camera button, then turned the phone so James could see Laurel and she could see him. Instantly, her face softened. Could she recognize his trademark bright green eyes as easily as Nolan had spotted hers, even at night?

"Is it really you, James?" Laurel asked, stepping closer as if she wanted to hug the phone to her heart.

"Yeah. Yeah, it's me." He burst into tears even when Laurel managed to hold it together. Jordan was there with his strong hand on James's back. "I've waited so many years for this moment. Are you okay? Where have you been? Can I help you at all? Please, let me make up for all the time I didn't know...." James hiccupped. "I didn't know."

"Where are you?" Laurel asked.

"Nolan will bring you here," James promised. "You can have faith in anything he tells you. He's one of the good guys. I swear on your doll with the floofy blue dress and blond hair that you gave me when you saw how much I loved it. I still have it, you know. I kept it for you."

Laurel shocked Nolan when she motioned for him to stand, caution evaporating, as if she couldn't wait another second after being separated from her little brother for decades. "Let's go."

"Pack a bag," Nolan told her. "Your essentials, in case you decide to stay for a bit. It's about a four- or five-hour drive from here."

She looked to Jace. "You're coming too, right?"

"Do you really have to ask?" He laced their fingers, cementing their relationship in Nolan's mind. "I'm not about to make the same mistake twice in one night. I'm with you."

Nolan sighed. What would it be like to have that kind of commitment? That kind of connection?

Someday he hoped to find out, but discovering the right pair of people to make his wildest dreams come true seemed about as unlikely as James being reunited with his long-lost sister instead of finding out that she hadn't made it or—maybe even worse—never knowing what had happened to her.

Except, that was about to go down.

Maybe sometimes miracles could be real.

5

L aurel tapped her foot on the floorboard. The repetitive motion wasn't enough to get rid of the nervous energy making it tough to draw in a full breath. It had been this way since they'd left their apartment, the only safe haven she'd ever known.

They flew through the dead of night in a black SUV with tinted windows. Even if they weren't in the middle of fucking nowhere, she doubted she'd be able to see much except for the pinprick starbursts of occasional passing headlights.

Jace scooted closer from where he sat beside her, Dottie's cage taking up the far side of the bench seat. He looped his arm around her shoulders and drew her to him so he could murmur in her ear. "You okay? I'll have them take us home or drop us off at a motel somewhere if you want to think more about this."

They'd been driving for hours already. Out of the industrial city perched on a polluted river not too close to the town she'd grown up in. It was the first time she'd been beyond its limits since Draven had imported her there. Even so, she'd been surprised when they'd turned onto the highway in the opposite direction from her hometown. Apparently James had moved west and that's where they were headed. There had been plenty of time—far too much, honestly—to mull over whether or not she was making a giant mistake.

Nolan didn't interrupt Jace or try to persuade him to stay the course. The woman with long brown hair swept into a tight ponytail and bright red lips who was driving, Sola, didn't so much as tap her brakes, but Laurel was sure they were listening for her response as eagerly as Jace.

Deep down, she believed if she told them that's what she'd chosen, they'd do it. And that made the decision for her.

"No. I want to see my brother. I'm just...anxious." Laurel didn't whisper. She couldn't say why, but she wanted Nolan's opinion on the matter. He seemed to know James pretty well, and there was something about him that fascinated her. His massive hands were capable of snapping her neck like a twig. He could have killed her earlier. Could have fought back when Jace jumped him. Could have turned the tables on them in their kitchen and done whatever he liked, she was sure of it.

The cut muscles of his core had rippled against her as he'd detained her firmly, but not roughly, and ushered her into the woods. At the time, she'd been terrified. Now she was curious about the kind of man who would do what he did. Stand up for what was right, even at the risk of his own safety. Against all odds, she wanted to have faith in him. Hope that there could be people that *good* and selfless—not to mention drop-dead gorgeous—in the world.

Which made him lethally dangerous to her.

Laurel had learned a long time ago not to let anyone sneak below her radar, especially not when they seemed to be doing her a favor, because the price was always greater than she cared to pay in the long run. Well, it had been with everyone but Jace. Their relationship was more reciprocal and, while completely fucked up, the closest thing she'd ever had to normal.

Peering at her in the darkness, he took her hand in his and chafed it. "What are you scared of?"

"What if I'm not what James expects?" She sighed. "It's been so long. I'm sure as hell not some naive girl anymore."

"You're right, you're not. You've been through enough to know that if he doesn't see you're a badass survivor, he doesn't deserve a place in your life, not even for a second to catch up. You say the word and we'll bail."

She nodded, then leaned on Jace, like she always did. The smell of his faux-leather coat reassured her, and she nuzzled his neck. Half of her wished they'd never seen that news report earlier while the other part remained optimistic that this could be the change they'd both been looking for lately. It had taken everything they'd had to scrape out of the pit they'd been thrown into as kids.

Somehow though, they'd done it. They'd endured, evolved, paid their way from under the phony debts Draven claimed they owed, then started putting together a new life. Hell, they hadn't had their electricity turned off in a couple years at least, and they even had a bit of savings for emergencies.

Now they were being transplanted into a new city, somewhere clean and fresh where Nolan had promised they could start over, if that's what they wanted. He'd been sparse on the details, but despite the alarms ringing in her mind, telling her not to put too much stock in a smooth-talking newcomer, a kernel of anticipation blossomed within her. That was most terrifying of all.

Laurel rolled the window down for a breath or two of crisp mountain air. Not a hint of smog or sewer or desperation in it.

"I'm good," she promised Jace before catching Nolan's gaze in the rearview mirror. He nodded subtly and smiled. Damn, even in the darkness, his teeth glowed bright and so did his ice-blue eyes. His blond hair swept back as if the wind had styled it. He might be a little high-maintenance compared to the kind of men she usually found attractive, but she couldn't deny he appealed to her.

Laurel probably should have felt weird about drooling over a dude while Jace held her, but whatever, it wasn't like he had any problems ogling the other guy either, or meeting up with strangers in shady places for a quick fuck. They didn't talk about it, but she knew he wasn't out for a run every time he came home sweaty and out of breath.

She supposed she could have done the same. After years of abuse and the meaningless sex she'd had on occasion afterward to raise some extra cash when they'd really needed it, she'd sworn to herself that she wouldn't. Instead, she'd strive to be spoiled enough that she only ever made love, on her terms, from then on out. And the one person—Jace—she'd been interested in exploring that entirely new facet of her sexuality with had never made a move nor responded to her subtle invitations.

"What?" He asked when she shot him a glare. "What'd I do?"

"Nothing." She sighed, because that was exactly the problem.

48

Nolan chuckled as if he could read her evident frustration, then said, "Hey, Sola, did Aarav head back with the rest of the team?"

"Yup. He told Jordan he'd wait with me for you, but the bossman told him to ride with Ransom, Levi, Marcus, and Kennedy instead. I guess they are already working on some of the intel they got from the victims to track down other branches of Draven's operation."

"I bet he was pissed, missing out on some quality time with you." Nolan waggled his brows causing Laurel to check Sola's reflection in the driver's side window. The woman winced, her eyes flicking to the edge of the road. Laurel hoped she hadn't cost Sola a chance alone with a friend or lover.

"He did seem more grumpy than usual." Sola shifted in the driver's seat, then smacked Nolan's thigh. "Quit gloating. I still think you're full of shit. He's not interested in me like that. The man hardly has any emotions. I can't see a robot like him having a damn crush on anyone, let alone me."

Jace snorted from beside Laurel. "Uh, I don't think that's so farfetched. Does he have eyes?"

Laurel didn't like the part of her that reared up, jealous over her roomie complimenting another woman. Jace was tough, but he could also be sweet.

"Thank you." Nolan twisted to look at Jace as if they were already on their way to being buds. "I bet Sola a hundred bucks one of our co-workers is into her. She doesn't believe me. But seriously, what guy stays late at work every day she's there unless it's because it's a convenient excuse to spend time with her?"

Jace did when Laurel's shifts at the restaurant went

late, though she figured his protective instincts didn't approve of her walking home in the dark.

"And always makes sure the command center fridge is stocked with her favorite drinks?"

Jace had splurged on Laurel's diet sodas even when they'd barely had a tap water budget.

"And is constantly watching her when she goes about her regular business?"

Laurel looked up at Jace, who shrugged sheepishly. He did all those things for her. Even in the dinner rush, she'd sometimes look up from taking an order to lock eyes with him across the room. And now she was doing it with Nolan, wondering who exactly he was teasing at the moment.

"Okay, okay. That's enough. Don't make things weird," Sola snapped at Nolan. "I love my job and I don't want anyone's boners messing that up for me."

That sounded like the truth if Laurel had ever heard it, but did it mean that Sola wasn't a little sad that she couldn't see if Nolan was right after all? Nope.

Laurel immediately regretted her prior envy. "Sometimes you have to sacrifice what you want to make sure you have what you need."

"I knew I was going to like you." Sola lifted one hand over the seat, beside the headrest, curled in a fist. Laurel bumped it. Damn it, she didn't want to give a shit about these people in case they were racing toward a disaster.

It wasn't too much longer before Sola turned into a well-lit entryway. Compared to the endless midnight engulfing them, it seemed like a beacon, drawing them closer. Really it turned out to be an illuminated stone sign that read "The Hawk's Nest" and a sleek guard shack at the center of very ornate metal gates.

Though it was pretty, Laurel held her breath. If it was that difficult to get in, it would be impossible for her to get out again if she changed her mind, and the Shields were not obliged to let her and Jace go. He tensed too. It was an all-too-familiar set up. When they'd been younger, before the cannery days, they'd been lent out to Draven's wealthier clients. Those who could afford fresh meat.

"Hold on," Laurel said, and wrapped her fingers around the door handle.

Sola immediately stopped and waited for her to elaborate. "Cold feet?"

"I'm not a fan of being locked in places." Laurel opened the window again and stuck her head out to let the cold air slap some feeling into her numb cheeks.

"Ah, shit. Sorry. I should have thought of that." Nolan tapped his phone, then said to whoever was on the other end of the line, "We're here, but going through the gates is freaking your sister out. Can we leave them unlocked? Otherwise we can divert and go to the cabin by the lake instead."

His courtesy alone relieved some of Laurel's anxiety. None of the people who'd used her or Jace had ever given a shit about their feelings or the trauma their actions would inflict.

"Whatever she wants," James responded. "Her friend too. I want them to be comfortable."

Laurel looked up at Jace, who nodded. She cleared her throat. "Let's go. It's okay."

"Jordan says they'll stay wide open until she says otherwise," the person who might be her brother promised Nolan. "When you're coming in, show her the path down the hill and how she could follow it to the lake if she ever feels she needs an escape route. There's no perimeter on that side of the estate."

"Will do. Thanks." Nolan disconnected, then turned in his seat to face her and Jace. "Are you ready?"

He wasn't rushing her either. The concern crinkling the corners of his eyes touched her. She looked at Jace. It wasn't only her who'd been enslaved before.

"I am if you are." He put his hand on the seat between them, palm up, and she laid hers over it, squeezing tight.

"I am too." Laurel drew a deep breath and was surprised to find she wasn't lying either. This was a moment she'd never been bold enough to even dream was possible. Even if there were some things that made her uncomfortable, she couldn't deny the excitement underlying her nerves. If she didn't care so much it would be easy to walk away.

But now that she was here, she couldn't.

Nolan smiled at her. Only then did Jace tell Sola to go ahead. The woman flicked her gaze to the rearview mirror, as if wanting to double check for herself that Laurel and Jace were okay before proceeding. It was another reinforcement that they were doing the right thing. Laurel had come to mistrust her own judgment after being shit on by pretty much everyone who'd ever supposedly had her back. Everyone but Jace.

They were still holding hands when they slid out of the SUV and stared up at the enormous mansion in front of them. Again, it reminded her of the estates where rich bastards who got off on buying kids had paid to turn them into party favors. It was beautiful with its mammoth chunks of stone, tree-trunk beams, and walls of glass in between, but she kind of hated it on sight.

True to his word, Nolan led them around the side of

the building and pointed out the spot where the moon glinted off the surface of a placid lake in the distance. "Like James said, there are no physical boundaries that way. Don't try to go straight down. It's steep and you could fall. Zigzag back and forth, descending at an angle. When you reach the shore, head west."

He pointed with his black leather glove in the correct direction. She wondered if he wore those when he worked to avoid leaving fingerprints. Odd that she had faith in a man who terminated others, but at least he was up front about it.

"It'll be a bit of a hike, but you'll cross the road and there's enough traffic to the lookout nearby that someone will probably spot you within an hour, tops, even at night."

Laurel hoped it never came to that, but she was grateful for the information just in case.

Nolan circled around to the main entrance and led them up flagstone stairs before letting them in to the mountain retreat. Immediately, a few things struck Laurel as different. There were no bodyguards watching the entrance and the people she could see inside were casually dressed, lounging around an enormous fireplace built of yet more boulders. They were laughing and joking, except for James, who sat in the middle of the group.

There was no doubt. She knew him right away.

From the moment his head whipped toward the door and their gazes locked, she was sure.

It was him. Her long-lost brother.

6

_____

Laurel's heart stuttered and her stomach dropped. Now that she was positive it was James, she cared what this beautiful man her brother had become thought of her. A whole lot more than she was comfortable with.

James's initial reflexive reaction wasn't to recoil with disdain or pity or disgust. Instead, he shot from the couch and dashed to her with a wide grin on his face. The dimples in his cheeks hadn't changed one bit since the last time she'd seen him, when he was only eight. Neither had his slightly unruly mop of brown hair with bright golden highlights that matched hers exactly. And though he was a grown man, he still had many of the boyish characteristics—overwhelming enthusiasm, a twinkle in his eye, and unfettered affection—she associated with her memories of him. He was a compact package of trim muscles with a tiny waist she was a bit envious of and he was only an inch or so taller than her.

But as he approached where she took a step forward and then another, he slowed a bit, nibbling his lower lip before he said, "I'm still a hugger, but I totally understand if that's not okay with you, Laurel-loo."

Laurel nearly choked on a half-laugh, half-sob. He was the only person who'd ever used that silly nickname for her. She flung herself at him and was surprised when her little brother caught her instead of tumbling to the ground beneath her forward momentum. He might not be anywhere near as tall as Jace or as thick as Nolan, but there wasn't an ounce of flab on his toned body. She wondered how a guy who rode desk kept in such good shape even if he worked for a private team of superheroes come to life.

For a few minutes they embraced and laughed, pure joy obliterating anything else. It didn't take too long before their initial gusto waned and the hard reality of what had torn them apart crept in, ruining the moment and everything good in her life, as it always did eventually.

She glanced over her shoulder at Jace, who was grinning, and then Nolan, who slung an arm around Sola. Both of them had sappy smiles plastered on their faces. Sola's gaze flicked to a man with dark, wavy hair who glared at Nolan with intense brown eyes and offered her a curt nod. Sola shrugged Nolan's heavy arm off her, then slipped toward the rest of the group by the fire. She sat between the guy Laurel would bet anything was Aarav and a relaxed, handsome Black man, who was beaming at Laurel and James.

That's when Laurel realized they were the center of an awful lot of attention.

Behind James, a tall man and a petite woman with short, straight blond hair approached, both with tears in their eyes. They had their arms wrapped around each other's waists and their stares locked on James. When her brother caught Laurel looking, he cleared his throat and introduced them.

"Sis, this is my wife, Devon, and my husband, Neil." James didn't so much as hesitate or blush as he gestured to the pair of people who apparently completed him.

"Oh. Wow." Laurel hadn't been normal in so long she hadn't even had time to imagine that James might be. That he could have a wife or, hell, even kids by now. And while she wouldn't have been the slightest bit shocked to learn that he was gay, it did sort of throw her for a loop to imagine that he was bisexual and polyamorous at that.

Most of all, it impressed her that he was so cool with exactly who he was. That alone made her prouder than she ever could have explained. Especially when she was such a fucking mess and had nothing of what she wanted most for herself.

Her gaze whipped to Jace then back. "That's..."

James's wife looked like she might rip Laurel's head right off if she said something to crush James at that moment, and Laurel instantly adored her sister-in-law. Laurel had done everything in her power to protect James when they were little. Knowing he still had people—bold, capable people—watching his back, meant he had chosen well.

"...amazing. I'm so happy you found your people."

Unlike James, Laurel wasn't usually into physical displays of affection, especially in public, but she didn't want any of them to mistakenly think—for even one moment—that she was some kind of close-minded asshole. She'd been through enough to be certain that what made someone good or evil had nothing to do with things like how many people they were married to, what their sexuality was, or how often they went to church. No, it had everything to do with how they treated the people around them, even when no one else was looking. So long as James and his spouses loved each other and treated each other right, she was happy—and maybe more than a little jealous—for all three of them.

She drew Devon and Neil to her, one in each arm, and patted their backs even if it was a bit awkwardly. "Thanks for taking care of James when I couldn't. Doesn't look like he needed my help after all, though."

So many nights she'd cried herself to sleep, not because she'd been ripped away from her family and trapped in hell, but because she was terrified that James had been too. She'd held her breath every time new workers were brought in to the dorm where she'd met Jace, terrified she'd see her brother among them.

They hugged her back when her breathing hitched and she turned to James once more.

"It was Uncle Rodger, wasn't it?" James asked, point-blank. Just hearing that sick fuck's name again made her knees wobble. "Wait, you don't have to answer that ever and definitely not in front of everyone, if you don't want to."

Jace was there on one side and Nolan on the other, to prop her up before she could fall.

James waved them toward the couches and the rest of the crowd, who'd gone dead silent while they had their reunion. Laurel wanted to rip free of the helping hands surrounding her waist, but she was so damn tired. Not only because it was the wee hours of morning and had been a hell of a day, but because the weight of everything she'd lived through came crashing down on her along with the memories they dredged up.

For once, she felt like it might be okay to rest for a moment. Surrounded by people who were supposedly decent human beings, her entire being relaxed...just a little.

Laurel murmured her thanks when Jace and Nolan ushered her to a soft, clean sofa that probably cost more than a year of rent on her and Jace's shabby apartment. She sank onto it and immediately thought it wouldn't be any hardship if she had to sleep on it, like Jace had so recently threatened to do with their three-legged, pokey-springed knock-off of this cloud in the shape of a seat.

Bookended by them, she felt strong enough to have the difficult conversation she knew was coming. James drew an ottoman over and perched on it, his husband and wife taking a seat nearby. He leaned in, his hands held out to her. She gladly accepted them, happy to be connected to him in the simplest of ways.

"Yeah. It was him. And I was terrified—every fucking minute—that I was going to turn around and find you there too. That he'd do to you what he'd done to me and then sell you off when you'd gotten too old for his liking or decided to start fighting back." Laurel hated to cry. Hadn't done it in a long fucking time before that night, but if she wasn't careful she was going to break down in front of all these outsiders and her brother, who was an odd mix of familiar and unknown.

"*Kuttar bachcha,*" the man sitting beside Sola grumbled. Laurel might not know whatever language he was cursing in, but she had no doubt that what he'd said wasn't meant for polite company. That was okay, she hadn't been delicate in a long damn time.

If that man was the Aarav who Nolan had been teasing Sola about in the car, Laurel figured Nolan was going to be a hundred bucks richer before too long. Sola raised her brow at him. Laurel thought maybe she might be realizing the guy wasn't as cold and unflappable as she had imagined.

"Laurel, I'm so sorry." James's lower lip wobbled a bit like it had those times he'd fallen off his bike and she'd put Band-Aids on his scratches. "You have to believe me. The cops told us you'd run away. That you'd come back if you wanted to. I didn't know, didn't even guess, until it was far too late. You took such good care of me, protected me, I had no idea how bad things were. I never would have stopped looking for you."

She squeezed his hands and looked dead in his eyes. "You were a kid, James. None of this is your fault."

"It was never yours either," Nolan said quietly, startling Laurel.

She almost argued, until she saw Jace's stern glare daring her to when he'd often said the same. Hearing it and believing it were two different things. She was working on it, but she wasn't quite there yet.

Instead, she shared something that none of them could argue with. "I *never* would have chosen to leave you behind. Not knowing what that monster was capable of and because...you were really the only true family I ever had. Mama, too, of course. But she was never around. You and me, though...we were always together. I would never have let that go without a fight."

Tears tracked down James's face. His husband and wife leaned in to console him even as Jace edged closer to her. She was surprised to see Nolan doing the same and even more shocked that his physical closeness, penning her in between him and Jace, didn't disturb her. She didn't usually like people infringing on her personal space.

Somehow, though, being sandwiched between these two particular men made her feel safe and protected during one of the most vulnerable moments of her life.

"I feel like such a shit. I was mad at you for a while, because you'd tossed me aside and abandoned me. I thought you must not have loved me like I thought. And all that time you were... I can't even think about it." He sobbed for them both.

"If it had to be one of us, I'm glad it was me." She wasn't lying either. James was softer than her. He might have given up, been broken like she'd nearly been so many times. She would gladly do it again to know that he'd been safe and happy and untouched.

"I love you, Laurel." James hugged her again. "Even when I was stupid and angry, that never stopped. I'm so glad to have you back."

"I love you too." It had been a lifetime since she'd uttered those words, never as an adult. Jace stiffened a bit beside her. She glanced over at him, wondering about the pained expression that flashed across his face before she returned her focus to James.

Had she hurt Jace by hiding the truth? By being too scared to admit that she cared for him too—as more than a friend or roommate or fellow survivor?

She'd have to fix that later.

For now, it unwound something deep inside her that her brother accepted her, without judgment, even having some idea of what she'd been forced to do. Maybe she was worthy of more than she thought.

"I hope that we can get to know each other again." Laurel stroked James's hair like she had those nights when he couldn't sleep and their mom worked the late shift, cleaning office buildings to make ends meet. "And Mom?"

She held her breath.

James shook his head once. "She had a heart attack in her sleep when I was seventeen. I know she wasn't around much, but it was because she thought providing was the best way to take care of us, and I think even though she didn't always know how to show it, she loved us very much. I'm pretty sure she suspected what her brother had done. After the police told us you weren't likely coming back and they were closing the case, we moved out to the suburbs where I met Neil and the rest of my crew. But she was never really the same again. As far as I know she never talked to that bastard again, and I think her heart was always broken after that. She went steadily downhill, fading away until one day she was just gone."

"So long ago," Laurel whispered, the loss fresh to her even if it was ancient history to James.

"I'm sorry," he said again.

"All this time I was afraid to search for you. I tried the old phone number once, a million years ago, and was so relieved when the recording said it had been disconnected. Didn't know what I would say, if I looked you two up. Draven told me no one gave a damn since no one ever came looking for me. It's hard to know what's real and what's not when you're in that environment. Everything is one giant mind fuck. Besides, he threatened to kill us if we ever talked about where we'd been after he let us out."

Laurel looked at the fire roaring in the hearth then because seeing James's reaction might be too much. It might crack her, and she had a feeling that if it did she wouldn't be able to put herself back together anytime soon.

Beside her Jace huffed, since they'd both agreed it was

best to leave the past alone. Did he have regrets too? How were they so close and yet so afraid to talk about the shit that mattered most? "The truth is, I was ashamed of what you would think. How she would react. And all this time it didn't matter. She was already gone."

"But I'm here, and damn sure you don't have a single thing to be self-conscious about."

Jace rubbed his thumb over her hand. Laurel focused on the repetitive motion to control the emotions that threatened to overwhelm her. Something James had said tingled her senses. She cleared her throat and diverted their discussion from territory that was still too painful and too raw. "Did you say, the *rest* of your crew? Do you have more spouses than these two?"

She tipped her head, fascinated and eager to learn about his life. A few of the Shields around them chuckled at that, easing the tension in the room from molar-cracking to merely ass-puckering.

"Uh, not exactly. But before I started working here with the Shields, I was a construction worker for the Powertools crew with Neil, Devon, and three other guys. We, and the rest of their wives, well...it's hard to explain but we've been through a lot together and we're more than friends."

"It might take me a minute to keep all this straight." Laurel shot him an apologetic grimace. "As long as you're content and they treat you well, you're lucky in my book."

James's gaze slid from her to Jace. He shot her roomie a lingering look that she recognized from a lot of men who were attracted to him. She would have swatted him, told him to back off and leave one stud for her, but she didn't have the right. It was too soon for that. And if James was waiting for her to explain her relationship with Jace, he was going to be disappointed. It wasn't anything she knew how to label.

From a spot near the fire, a man with sandy hair and a no-nonsense set to his strong jaw crossed his arms and cleared his throat. Everyone snapped to attention.

7

———

Laurel's throat went dry. It was obvious the guy had a lot of power and influence, and with this group that said a lot. She was sure she owed him for bringing her and James back together, never mind whatever was to come next.

James, however, grinned. "Oh, yeah. That's our boss, Jordan. He's the founder and head of the Shields."

"I'm glad to be meeting you in person. We figured it was a long shot, but I'm glad fortune—and Nolan's dumb ass—worked out in our favor today. He said you took him to your place. When James ran the address, it didn't come up as one of Draven's known holdings. Can I ask how you were able to leave his organization?"

Jordan tipped his head a bit, and she felt that if she said no, he wouldn't pressure her. For that matter, she realized that behind his left shoulder the television was displaying footage from a security camera, which clearly —and for her benefit, she was sure—showed the live image of the wide-open gates. After all he'd done for them, she figured she owed him at least that much. Besides, he was the kind of man who'd find out one way or another. So she nodded.

"We bought our way out. There came a time where we were worth more to Draven working at Heels than being rented because of our ages and the fact that Jace had a tendency to fight back even if some people took pleasure in his struggles." Laurel grimaced.

Jace added, "He told us what our freedom would cost and we worked it off. It took more than ten years, but we did it. Laurel dancing and me bouncing, Draven taking everything but crumbs. Barely enough for us to survive on our own. And after we paid him we swore to keep a low profile, because he said he'd kill us and whatever family we had left if we didn't."

"Until tonight, we kept our word." Laurel smiled sadly at James. "After meeting Nolan, I figured that if he was telling the truth about you and your team here, then you'd be plenty capable of taking care of yourself."

"Son of a bitch. I hate that they used me against you." James slapped a fist into his open palm. "And I love you for giving a shit about me even after everything you've been through."

"You'll always be my little brother."

James whispered, "You'll always be my big sis. You know you were a huge part of the reason I wanted to do this. Seeing how our bullshit excuse for a justice system operates, I knew the Shields could do better, even if our work is outside those bounds."

Laurel swallowed the knot in her throat. He'd still been thinking of her despite all the years in between them. Even after he knew what she'd become.

"Sometimes you've got to use their methods against them to win. In the end, Jace had to persuade Draven to finally go through with it, and we've been laying low since."

"What does that mean exactly?" Jordan asked with too-keen eyes.

"I threatened to stab him with a giant chef's knife I'd stolen from the kitchen for just such an occasion." Jace had not an ounce of remorse in his grim smirk. "And I would have gladly slit his throat if he'd tried to stop us from walking out that door."

"Fair enough." Jordan shrugged. "I might have done it anyway to keep him off my ass, and because he deserves it. I'm impressed with your self-restraint."

"Yeah, we looked over our shoulders a lot in the beginning, but he must have been convinced we were too afraid to cause him any trouble and he left us alone." Jace shrugged.

"Okay, now I have a question." Nolan turned to Laurel and Jace, his hand half-raised. He was awfully earnest and adorable considering what he did for a living. "If you worked so damn hard to get out of that mess, what were you doing creeping around Heels tonight?"

"We saw the cannery raid on the news." Jace pinched the bridge of his nose as if that was a million years ago instead of only a few hours. "James's sis here decided she needed to get the scoop on what went down from some of our old friends in case she could help anyone else get away."

"If I'd known you'd already done such a terrific job of it, I would have stayed snuggled in bed with Jace." On the way to their command center, which was apparently somewhere in this monstrous mansion, Nolan had reassured them the rest of the workers had been seen to and would never be victims of Draven again.

Nolan raised his brows at her inadvertent disclosure. She ignored him. Their sleeping arrangement wasn't as fun as he was imagining, she was sure. Comforting, reliable, secure...yep. Boom chicka wow wow, nope.

"But then you wouldn't have been found," James murmured. "Thank God Nolan happened to spot you."

"Got lucky, being in the right place at the right time, even if you didn't appreciate it immediately." Nolan winked at her despite the purple shadow she could see on his poor jaw. She sat on her hand to keep from stroking it with her thumb.

"Yeah, about that...I'm sorry I knocked your ass out," Jace grumbled. "But when I saw you grab Laurel, I assumed the worst."

Laurel turned to Jace and tipped the side of her head onto his shoulder. "Thanks. I was dumb not to wait for you."

"Wait. Nolan was unconscious?" asked a young woman with blond hair, blue eyes, and fair skin, who'd been sitting quietly on the arm of the sofa next to the handsome Black man with a well-trimmed beard, waves shaved into the sides of his fade, and bold diamond stud earrings. Shooting Jace a glare, she propped a hand on her slender hip and crossed to them.

"Uh. Yeah, sorry." Jace gave a sheepish half-smile. "I didn't realize he was on our side at first. He grabbed Laurel and dragged her into the woods..."

He shrugged. Laurel got the feeling anyone else in the room would have done the same in his situation. Maybe worse.

Nolan said, "Totally understandable. No hard feelings, man."

"Has anyone checked you out? How long were you down for?" the woman asked, making Laurel wince. These people weren't savages, like her and Jace. They probably hadn't lived in a world where you were used, abused, then discarded like trash and left to heal on your own. Where no one gave a shit if you were damaged unless it meant they couldn't charge as much for you next time.

Ironically, her and Jace aging out and becoming less desirable had been what had ended up saving them. If she'd known that, she'd have made herself worthless a lot sooner.

"Nah. No need. I'm fine, Kennedy." Nolan rubbed the stubble on his jaw, which did look a bit puffier on one side than the other, and almost concealed his wince. "Probably just a bruise. At least it's not a shiner, huh? Won't mess up my game too much."

He winked at them.

Laurel snorted at that because Nolan knew exactly how hot he was and so did everyone else who looked at him. Jace included. She'd seen the way her best friend eyed the agent, and she didn't blame him one damn bit. Nolan was attractive, confident, and utterly capable.

But no match for Jace's raw passion and underlying righteous rage, which simmered near the surface.

Whew. Laurel fanned her face, pretending it was the fire or her nerves making the room so steamy when she damn well knew it was the two men she was wedged between.

The woman, though her pink lips were still pinched with concern, turned to Laurel and Jace and stuck out her hand. "I'm sorry this dumbass scared you. Sometimes I swear he's like a big goofy dog who gets out of the gate but only to charge up to the mailman and lick his face."

"I mean, is it a smokin' mailman, maybe young and fit from walking his route in a pair of gray-blue uniform pants?" Nolan grinned even if it was a tad lopsided given the swelling in his cheek.

Jace whipped his gaze to Nolan while James hummed appreciatively at the mental image.

The woman, however, rolled her eyes. "Yeah, I see he's acting entirely normal. Anyway, I'm Kennedy. I'm a doctor and the medic on most of our missions. I was treating the victims at the cannery while Nolan wandered off. You know if you'd waited for Sola, you probably wouldn't have gotten laid out."

"But then I would have missed Laurel and Jace." Nolan stretched his jaw. "They're pretty cool. And I didn't even have to take out anyone at the club to get them here. I'd say it was worth it. Now the shot to the nuts, that's another matter."

Laurel couldn't help but laugh with a shake of her head despite the circumstances. Jace snorted too. She choked on her, "Sorry."

The rest of the Shields and James's spouses cracked up.

It was officially one of the weirdest and most amazing nights of her life. How could everything have changed so fast and yet seem so perfect? It wasn't a feeling she was used to, and it kind of freaked her out. She entwined her fingers with Jace's and looked on as Kennedy examined Nolan.

The doc shined a pencil-thin flashlight into Nolan's eyes, making them practically glow neon blue. Damn. To avoid staring, Laurel glanced around the room, really taking in each of the agents surrounding them for the first time. It didn't bother her to have people looking at her. She'd grown numb to being a spectacle long ago, and had sort of learned to block out unwanted attention. But now that she was inspecting each of James's coworkers, who were obviously also friends, she started to feel a bit shy about laying out their private business in front of so many onlookers.

James jumped up and started talking superfast. "Oh shit. Let me introduce you to the rest of the team. Don't worry if you can't remember their names. There are a lot of us, I know."

He started with the people left on the couch Kennedy had abandoned. "You know Sola. This is Aarav, and that's Marcus."

Laurel tried to imagine the bearded man with the steady gaze as a sniper and she could see why Sola might mistake him for emotionless, though she sensed he was keeping at least as much bottled up inside as she was. The other guy lifted his chin in greeting, but didn't say anything, his gaze somewhere in the region of Kennedy's ass if Laurel's estimation proved correct.

Interesting. All sorts of sensual currents were flowing around this place, making Laurel acutely aware of the hard male thighs—one Jace's familiar one and one Nolan's thicker model—pressed to each of hers.

"These guys are Ransom and Levi," James pointed to a pair of men sharing the last couch in their U-shaped set up. "And of course you met Jordan. His husband and wife are around here somewhere too."

"Damn." Jace whistled under his breath as he scanned the room. "Is there something in the water in that lake or what?"

Ransom looked to Levi and grinned. "I'm not sure. I'll ask our wife, Sevan, later."

Laurel blinked. The ups and downs of the night, reuniting with James, meeting everyone, and having her mind blown over and over was starting to wear on her.

She yawned, scrubbing her eyes.

"Ah, shit. It's practically dawn. There are a million rooms here if you want me to show you to one." James waved toward the balcony above that apparently led to private quarters.

She looked to Jace. Whether he could feel the apprehension radiating off of her or he felt the same, he shook his head no subtly.

"I really, really appreciate the offer, but I'm not comfortable in a place like this." Laurel fidgeted, toying with the hem of her sweater. "It's incredible and you're all so lovely and kind, but it reminds me of party houses we used to be taken to—"

James's husband, Neil, cursed beneath his breath and James waved away the rest of her statement. "Nope. No way. We're not going to make you relive that. I have a much better idea."

He turned to Jordan. "I'll take them to Hot Rides. Since Joy, Walker, and Dane moved into the bigger place Dave just finished building for them, there's an empty tiny home on site. It has two bedrooms so—as long as Kennedy clears him and my sis and Jace are cool with it— Nolan can stay with them. The Hot Rides will be happy to help him watch their backs for a while. They'll be as safe as here but more comfortable."

"A damn fine suggestion." Jordan nodded. "For the record, my spouses and I have a place there too. It's a motorcycle garage. My wife, Wren, is their welder. We stay there most times during the week so I can help Nolan with shifts too."

"For the record, he's going to be fine. Nothing some anti-inflammatories and a few days won't fix." Kennedy chose then to finish her exam of Nolan and patted his cheek, making him grunt. She returned to her perch beside the man with the wave shaved into his onyx hair. Sola and her buddy Aarav studied Laurel with an expression she took for resignation and maybe empathy. She figured Jordan always got his way.

"Wait. What?" Laurel looked to Jace then back to James. A house? Nolan living with them? Everyone else bunking there had multiple spouses too? It was a lot to digest. So she started with the simple facts first. "We can't stay here. We have to go to work tomorrow. We don't get vacation time and if we bail with no notice we'll be fired for sure. We need our jobs."

"Laurel-loo." James winced. "You can't go back. We pissed Draven off big time and we're not going to stop with kicking this one hive. Not when we have hard evidence about what's going on and, well, uh..." He studied his cute yellow sneakers.

"What your brother is dancing around is that we really need you to be informants if we're going to shut this shit down for good." Jordan spread his legs wider, as if this time he wouldn't take no for an answer.

The gates might be open, but Laurel felt the walls closing in around her regardless. Jace must have too. He sprang to his feet and said, "No. Absolutely not."

"Tell me again why you two were lurking in the shadows at Heels tonight?" Jordan asked with a single raised brow. Laurel knew his type—cool on the outside and fiery down deep—they were the most dangerous.

But he was making it hard to argue.

"Right. Okay. I see what you mean. I *do* want to help and keep anyone else from going through what we have. I'd like for this to be over. For good." Laurel sighed. "Is this the best way?"

Jace whipped around and stared at her like he had when she'd proposed running off to Heels earlier before slicing his hands through the air. "Are you serious right now? You'd throw away our jobs, our home—shitty as it is, it's ours—and the future we were getting so close to, for the promise of something we both know is fucking impossible? Cops haven't ever nailed that bastard. Why would your brother's friends be able to pull it off?"

Okay. That was legit too. "Jace is right, you know. There were plenty of times police officers and politicians laughed at the idea of getting caught, never mind stopped. The kind of money Draven has makes him exempt from the law."

"Funny thing about that," Nolan said. "We don't operate within the rules either."

Aarav nodded and spoke up for the first time. "This is exactly why we do what we do. To put things right when they're unjust. To take back power when the balance has shifted."

Marcus agreed. "If you work with us, we won't stop until Draven and his organization are no longer a problem. Not only for you, but for everyone else too. It's the only way you'll ever really be able to stop looking over your shoulder."

That sounded like heaven. No, like peace. And it had been a long damn time since Laurel thought that was possible to have. She looked up at Jace, her eyes wide, silently begging him to see things their way.

"What if this blows back on us? I don't give a shit about myself, but I swear, if anything happens to you, I'm not going to stop at knocking people out." He clenched his fists and swung around, glaring at every last person around them, James and Nolan included.

Laurel stood and approached Jace from behind. She put her arms around him, laid her palms flat on his chest and her cheek on his back. She held him until his breaths slowed and grew less ragged. She went on her tiptoes to whisper in his ear. "We're going to be okay, Jace. This is the future we didn't know we could have. Everything could change for us and for so many other people. It's worth the risk."

"How are we going to afford this place?" Jace looked over his shoulder, then back to Jordan. "We have a little bit saved up, but not much and Laurel was going to use it for college. It's going to take a minute to get work. Are there any restaurants around? Or maybe I could gig? I play guitar and sing. I'm pretty sure I don't totally suck."

"It's okay, Jace—" Laurel was about to offer up her college fund.

"Oh. That's not an issue." Jordan waved their concerns aside. "Being an informant pays better than most of the jobs in Middletown, the place James is proposing for you. And the house we have there is empty at the moment. The Powertools, James's construction buddies, use it as a model for people wanting to hire them to build tiny homes, or she-sheds, or whatever."

"Thank you, but I don't really like the idea of being beholden to anyone else." Laurel recoiled, but she only knocked into Nolan, who had also risen. The warm, solid mass of him didn't make her feel any less trapped. Jace was shaking his head too.

"I can understand where you're coming from." Jordan paused. "As I said, you will be paid members of our team. Your insights and information are very valuable and you'll be compensated well for sharing them. But if you like, Devra—the wife of the owner of Hot Rides, where you'll be staying—owns a restaurant in town. She's always looking for reliable servers, and my husband probably has use for a musician."

Jace paused but still seemed skeptical. "Does he travel for work? I won't leave Laurel alone at night."

Laurel hated to admit it but the security blanket of Jace's company was very welcome. Especially in a new place, with a man she just met in the other room, she would probably freak out if she didn't have Jace nearby.

"Ummm, yeah, he does when he's on tour, which he's not right now. He was talking about getting someone to play backup guitar for his jam sessions while he's writing new music. That could happen here or even at Hot Rides if you're decent enough to free him up from playing while he's coming up with new lyrics and can help him test out harmonies," Jordan said with a somewhat dreamy smile that shattered his tough-guy demeanor.

"Jace is beyond *decent*. He's incredible." Laurel might be unsure about a lot of the stuff happening at the speed of light around them, but that wasn't one of them. If things had been different, Jace would have been signed to a record label a long time ago, she was certain of it.

"Then I'm sure Kason will be happy to hire him. See. No problems." Jordan spread his hands out wide in front of him.

Jace squinted at the elaborate mansion they were huddled in, then back to Jordan. "Hold on. Who exactly is your husband? Someone I would know?"

Everyone burst out laughing, but not in a malicious way. Jordan smiled kindly and nodded. "Kason Cox. The country star."

"Oh. Holy shit." Jace plopped down on the couch again and Laurel joined him. He looked over at her and she could see him struggling, at war within himself. This was a dream opportunity for him, everything else aside.

Laurel took his hand and said, "Let's do it. Let's stay."

He bit his lower lip then looked over at Nolan. "I'm afraid this is sounding too good to be true and that it will turn out to be a giant cluster fuck, but... If you're willing to gamble, I am too."

"You were the one talking about our future and how we needed to be brave and go for it if we're ever going to do better. We're running out of time day by day, getting older. So much was stolen from us, we've got a late start. I'm ready to be bold. To believe that things can be different and that we've had enough bad luck to deserve a break. Maybe this is it..."

Jace sighed, paused, then nodded. "Okay. I'm in."

Laurel flung herself into his arms and laughed out loud, the peal ricocheting around the room when he caught her and cradled her to his chest. She peeked from beneath his arms—which banded around her, sheltering her as always—at James. Her brother grinned and leaned against his husband as his wife settled onto his lap and kissed the trail of his, hopefully happy, tear.

Grateful, Laurel looked around the room at Jordan, Sola, Aarav, Kennedy, Marcus, the two big guys—Ransom and Levi—and, of course, her brother with his spouses. In one evening, she felt like she might have gained an entire new family of sorts. That terrified her. It had been a long damn time since she'd had to care—or worry—about anyone but herself or Jace.

And, hell, she still couldn't seem to sort things out quite right with him after decades of trying.

Finally, she looked at Nolan and slow blinked at the heated gaze he was shooting her and Jace. One filled not with pity but with longing. She'd seen desire often enough to recognize it immediately. But unlike nearly all the other times it had been aimed in her direction, she didn't feel like running away.

Instead, she leaned closer. "Sorry 'bout your luck, roomie. I'm pretty neat, but Jace...he's a slob."

"Hey, I wash my own clothes and almost always remember to put the toilet seat down." He squeezed her, then laughed. "I guess there will be no more walking around naked after your showers, though—that's gonna be a bummer."

"Why? I certainly won't object." Nolan was quick to flash them a grin. "Hell, I'm not a big fan of clothes and I don't even own pajamas."

"Old habits are hard to break." Laurel shrugged one shoulder. She couldn't say what got into her. Maybe it was pure exhaustion making the filter between her brain and her mouth dissolve. Or maybe it was the thrill it gave her to be in Jace's arms while another man stared at her hungrily. Or maybe a teensy part of her wanted Jace to know what it was like to be jealous considering she was practically a born-again virgin though he indulged in periodic hookups.

No matter what, it was going to be an interesting couple of months until Jordan could nail Draven and end a very long, very ugly chapter of their lives permanently.

Marcus chuckled, then said, "Why do I feel like Nolan has no idea what he's getting himself into?"

Kennedy tapped him on the shoulder with the back of her hand and cackled. "I'm sure you're right and I can't wait for him to find out."

Neither could Laurel.

8

The first few days Nolan spent with Jace and Laurel had flown by in a flash. He'd arranged for someone on the team to collect the rest of their stuff from their apartment. Shockingly few boxes of simple necessities had arrived later that same day. It was probably for the best given the limited storage in the tiny home they were sharing at Hot Rides, though Jace and Laurel acted like they'd hit the lottery and moved into a mansion.

Strike that. They hadn't cared much for Jordan, Kason, and Wren's sprawling mountain palace. But Nolan had seen Laurel sigh as she ran her fingers over the gleaming stainless faucet in the kitchen sink and the glossy surface of the marble island. With a compact space, the Powertools crew had easily incorporated bits of luxury in the tiny homes they'd built on the Hot Rides campus.

If Nolan was being honest, he didn't mind the close quarters. It meant he got to spend all of his time getting to know his charges really fucking well. Ordinarily, he'd be bitter about being slapped on babysitting duty. All of the

Shields knew it was Jordan's way of spanking him for taking off to investigate Heels on his own the night of the raid.

Though he'd grumbled to the team, he had to keep reminding himself not to completely fuck up and let his guard down, because living with Laurel and Jace, watching over them, was as natural as breathing.

Just that morning, he'd tried to hide a smirk behind his napkin when Laurel had busted Jace's balls while they ate breakfast on stools at the kitchen peninsula that doubled as a table.

"Sugar Shreds? Really? What are you, ten?" Laurel rolled her eyes as she cut up a banana to add to the blueberries already topping her oatmeal.

"Definitely never had stuff like this when I was a kid." He shrugged.

Nolan tried not to cringe. No, little references like these made him pretty sure Jace had been dumpster diving to survive back then. "Hey, you're never too old to enjoy a bowl of half-candy cereal. Pour me some?"

Nolan erased any lingering awkwardness by joining in. And even if the stuff was nasty, it was worth choking it down to see Jace's less-rare these days smile. He'd have to run an extra five miles later but he'd live.

Laurel reached over and squeezed Nolan's knee under the bar, which made it an even more worthwhile sacrifice. Somehow he had fallen into this role, smoothing over the unintentional emotional paper cuts they inflicted on each other, and he didn't mind one bit.

They cracked him up when they dealt a bit of shit. Impressed him with their resilience, taking everything that had happened in stride and rolling with their new reality. Finding joy in things others would easily overlook while playing down the bad shit that came their way. He figured dogged positivity was a skill they'd had to learn early on to survive in Draven's empire. He couldn't think about that for long or he'd grab his gun and fuck up their entire well-thought-out mission in a flare of rage he didn't often experience.

On top of that, they were innocently making him jealous as fuck as he witnessed their incredible intimacy. Hell, they were constantly touching each other. Even now they were cuddled up on the couch as Jace hummed a melody he and Kason had been working on in their first session the day before. His fingers idly combed through Laurel's damp hair, which he'd dried with a fuzzy-as-fuck towel after refusing Nolan's offer to scrounge up a blow dryer from one of their new neighbors. He'd said he didn't want to impose, but Nolan wouldn't blame the guy if he'd simply wanted to touch Laurel's silky locks and encourage her soft moans as he massaged her scalp in the process.

Plus, there was the way they slept together.

Nolan would never admit to the rest of the Shields how much of each night he'd spent staring at the two of them wrapped in each other's arms as the moonlight streamed through their window. The truth was, they were so damn exhausted they'd slept for more than twelve hours each of the first three days they'd been under his watch. His shoulders went back and his chest puffed up knowing they'd relied on him to keep them safe when they passed out, the weight of their responsibilities temporarily lifted from Jace's ripped and tattooed shoulders and worry erased from Laurel's soul.

Maybe that's why Nolan was drawn to them, more every moment they spent together. They tripped his protector instincts. Or maybe it was because they were so damn appreciative for every tiny kindness their new friends in Middletown, who were quickly knitting themselves into an iron-clad support system, showed them. Their dazed wonder at simple decency made Nolan realize exactly how much he'd taken for granted in his life. So he'd arranged for a few surprises.

He paced the floor of the bungalow he shared with his two new obsessions, crossing from the kitchen through the living room and to the front door all too quickly. He couldn't wait for them to see what he and James had been cooking up and hoped he wasn't about to make a fool out of himself.

Though it would be worth it if he earned one of Laurel's wide smiles or Jace's fist bumps.

Right on time, as always, a triple tap came at the door. "Yoohoo, it's me. James."

Laurel grinned and bounded the handful of steps between the couch and the entryway to let him in. Nolan stepped in front of her, wrapping his arm around her waist to keep her from bouncing off of him and into the fireplace. He'd been careful not to touch her, afraid of spooking her or invading her personal space. To his surprise, she didn't recoil, so he left his hand splayed on her lower back, ignoring the glare that Jace shot him from the couch.

"I'm sure it's fine, but why don't you let me do that?"

"Oh. Right." The corners of Laurel's eyes tightened, making Nolan want to put his boot up his own ass. A sense of security didn't come naturally for either Laurel or Jace, so knowing they were already growing comfortable in Middletown, surrounded by their allies and in his presence, did something funny to his insides.

That didn't mean he was taking any damn chances. No, it meant he'd be extra careful.

He reluctantly released Laurel, then rested his hand on the grip of the gun tucked in his shoulder holster instead. Nolan glanced out the door. James flashed him the all-clear hand signal and there was no indication of any unwanted visitors on the gently winding path behind him that led from their sanctuary to the Hot Rides motorcycle shop in the background.

"It's fine," he promised Laurel, then grinned as he flung the door open and yanked James inside. Oops. Sometimes he forgot the guy was shorter and more slender than most of the Shields. He certainly didn't act weaker in any way.

But his manhandling was nothing compared to Laurel's welcome. She flung herself at her baby brother and wrapped her arms and legs fully around him. James laughed and shoved the package he was carrying at Nolan so he could catch Laurel instead. "I missed you too."

"It's still such a rush. Every time I see you, my heart is happier." Laurel kissed his cheek, and slid down until her toes touched the ground again. Then she noticed the wooden box he'd set on the ground before knocking. "What's that?"

Nolan held his breath.

"It's a new house for Dottie." James beamed. "It seems only fair to upgrade her too."

"You built our lizard a castle?" Laurel's eyes went wide and misted over. "That's so...sweet."

"I can't take all the credit. It was Nolan's idea, I followed his plans. With a few embellishments, of course." James picked up the cage and brought it inside, setting it on the counter top. "I mean, what lizard doesn't enjoy a red rock tanning bed or a stick maze with a leaf hammock, am I right?"

Nolan had to admit it looked even more impressive than he'd imagined based on the stream of texts he'd been exchanging with James.

Laurel bounded into the bedroom she shared with Jace, then emerged with Dottie riding her shoulder. She opened the front gate and leaned toward it. Dottie hopped into the cage, her really impressive tongue flicking out as she explored every nook and cranny of the space, just like Laurel had the bright kitchen and claw-foot tub in the tiny home.

From the couch, Jace grunted. "Make sure there's nothing she can get hurt on in there."

"There's not. It's perfect." Laurel beamed at James and then aimed the sun-strength wattage of her smile in Nolan's direction.

"I could probably have made her a better cage if we'd had the resources." Jace crossed his arms over his chest, adorably defensive and grumpy. Nolan thought he had just the cure. Well, one that would be professionally acceptable as opposed to kissing the pout right off his sexy lips.

"I'm sure you could have." James smiled kindly, though Nolan figured there was no way someone could have crafted a masterpiece like Dottie's cage on command without the decades of skilled experience James had from his previous career working for Powertools, and a hell of a lot of natural talent. Which Jace had too, when it came to music.

Nolan cleared his throat, feeling even less certain about his choices now. "I, uh, had something for you too. Hopefully, you'll like it better than Dottie's cage."

He caught James's subtle shake of his head a little too late. The words had already spilled from his mouth and he was standing there with the box in his hands, extended toward Jace.

"What's this?" Jace looked up at Nolan, his eyes dark and wary.

"Open it and find out." His heart beat unexplainably loudly as Jace took the package and uncovered the guitar case inside.

Rich and supple, the midnight blue leather of the custom carrier looked even more striking in person than it had in the pictures Kason had sent him while they were browsing online together at some outrageous shop Kason bought his own instruments from.

Jace popped it a crack, then froze before slowly pushing the lid all the way open and setting it gently on the coffee table as he cradled the main compartment in his lap.

James whistled. "Damn. I can tinker with lizard cages all day long, but I could never create something like that. How the hell do they get it so shiny?"

"What is this?" Jace's gaze shot to Nolan, and Laurel gasped.

"I thought you knew how to play," Nolan teased. "It's a guitar."

"It's a work of art." Now it was Jace's turn to lovingly stroke something.

Nolan's cock twitched in his jeans as the man ran one fingertip along the curve of the glossy Brazilian rosewood as he stared longingly at the guitar. Nolan cleared his throat and said, "It's for you. Those songs you sing deserve to be played on something like this. You're good. You're *really* good."

Then Jace doused Nolan in ice water. "I can't accept this."

"Of course you can." Nolan waved off his rejection. "If you think informants get paid a ton, you should see how many zeros are on the checks Jordan passes out to the people who put their lives on the line for the Shields."

James cleared his throat, cluing Nolan in to the fact that he was only making things worse. "I'm not bragging, I'm saying it's not that big of a deal to me and I thought you might like it."

Laurel smiled sadly at Nolan. He knew right then Jace wasn't going to keep his gift. She understood Jace a lot better than he did, and Nolan would do well never to forget that again. He should have asked her about this first.

Jace shut the lid of the guitar case extra carefully for a man who was distinctly rough around the edges. He touched it like he did Laurel, reverently. But when he looked up at Nolan, his eyes were almost hollow and his voice flat, nothing like when he sang. "Thanks, but I'm used to my guitar. It might not be flashy, it's full of scratches and scars, but it fits me. Unless Kason said mine sounds like shit on his session recordings or something."

"No. No, of course he didn't." James tried to smooth things over, which was usually Nolan's job. Damn it, he'd fucked up. "He was so excited when he went home to Jordan last night he made us all listen to what you were working on about five hundred times on repeat. I'm no expert, but it was so catchy I talked him into letting me download the recording to my phone to listen to in the car on the ride home. You're a true artist."

"Thanks." Jace nodded, then sighed as he slid the guitar a few inches away.

"Sorry. I didn't mean to shit on your set up." Nolan barely bit back a curse.

James laid his fingers on Nolan's wrist, but he shook them off and reached for the guitar, wishing he could hide it out of sight.

"No worries. We're good." Jace's smile was tight, though. "It's just...That's over the top. You guys have done so much for us already. I've got to earn something. Be worth it, you know?"

"You are." Nolan was shocked. Who would think they weren't deserving of kindness?

Jace stared back without blinking, clearly not convinced.

Laurel was there, rubbing his back in a slow circle, nodding. "Thank you. For Dottie's cage. For thinking of Jace. For everything. It's kind of overwhelming. We're not used to people being so generous without asking something in return. Sometimes more than we'd like to give."

Ah, fuck. The last thing Nolan wanted was to make either of them feel indebted. Or like he was going to call on them for favors—sexual or otherwise—to repay him. He'd gone too far. He'd only wanted to help. And to see them smile. Somehow he'd done exactly the opposite. Damn it!

"Well, I'll put this over here. And someday if you decide to buy it off me, I'll give you a good deal." Nolan shrugged as if the rejection of his gift didn't sting a bit, even though he understood he'd mashed Jace's buttons. "Not bad to have a spare on hand when Kason's over anyway, right?"

"Yeah. Yeah, that sounds good." Jace settled a bit.

It took an hour of Laurel and James shooting the shit,

infecting the whole place with their light and laughter, before Jace fully unwound. Nolan was grateful to the other guy for sticking around and patching his slip up. But eventually the light started to fade and James checked his watch.

"Gotta go play house husband?" Nolan teased, figuring acting like an asshole was about as normal as he got.

"Devon and Neil will be home soon. I like to be there to feed them and help them relax after a long day on their sites." James had found his happy place where he could take care of his spouses and do something fulfilling for himself.

"Is that code for hot threesomes?" Jace lifted his brows and Nolan laughed. Maybe things would be okay after all. "Or maybe more with the rest of that crew of yours?"

Laurel slapped him on the shoulder. "I do not want to know about my brother's sex life, thank you."

"You can tell me later." Jace high-fived James, who promised to kiss and tell.

Nolan did not need to hear about that steaminess right then. Not with Laurel and Jace nearby and his emotions still sort of ragged. "I'll walk you out."

James hugged Laurel and then Jace too. While he seemed surprised at first, his stiff arms embraced James after a second. James patted Jace's back, then whispered something Nolan couldn't hear. Jace nodded and smiled. "Thanks again."

"Anytime. See you two tomorrow. Nolan, walk me out?" James waved as they slipped out the door and headed for James's ridiculous, pint-sized, neon-green electric car, which seemed like it belonged on the crowded streets of Europe or something rather than in the parking lot of a badass motorcycle shop.

"Sorry that didn't go the way you hoped." James winced.

"Win some, lose some." Nolan shrugged, though he wasn't as unfazed as he tried to act. He'd started to think there was something magical about Middletown. Everywhere he looked, people were happy, in love—with more than one person even—and he'd started to believe maybe he'd get lucky enough to stumble across his perfect people too. "Thanks anyway for all you did organizing everything and picking it up."

"No problem." James hugged Nolan as warmly as he had Laurel and Jace, squeezing him tight before pulling away. "Give them time, Nolan. They'll learn who you are, but you're going to have to be patient or you'll scare them away."

Could James tell how attracted he was to both of his temporary roommates? And was he going to rat Nolan out to their boss? He'd have to be more careful to hide his feelings when they had no place on the job. "I've got an assignment, and that's all I'm worried about here."

"You're cute when you're in denial." James rolled his eyes. "Maybe I'm going to go make a bet with Sola like the one you made with her about Aarav. It'll be easy money."

Nolan's eyes bugged out. "Don't."

"Just kidding. Your secret is safe with me." James winked. "Besides, you couldn't handle her ragging on your ass like you do to her."

Fuck again. Nolan realized in an instant that his teasing might not be quite as hysterical as he'd assumed. Not when there were real feelings involved. The stakes somehow seemed higher. It wasn't funny. So he swore then and there he'd never make a joke of the smoldering tension between his co-workers—Sola and Aarav or Marcus and Kennedy, for that matter—ever again.

"I might not be perfect, but I hear you and I'll work on it," Nolan promised James.

"Good. Because if anyone upsets my sister, they're going to have to answer to me."

Nolan coughed, hoping it disguised his chuckle, because he didn't put it past James to make his life miserable in the most resourceful ways possible. He held his hands up, palms out. "Got it. Loud and clear."

"Perfect. Have a good night!" James gave Nolan one of his patented finger waves, then flounced down the path, humming the song Jace and Kason had co-written the day before.

9

J ace stretched. When Laurel hummed in her sleep and snuggled closer to him, he kissed her forehead, then disentangled them before she roused fully. His raging erection would be impossible to hide. It had been more than two weeks since they'd started sharing this new, unsaggy, and broken-spring-free bed. He'd been playing music with a mega-star every day and getting paid more in a month than he had in a year at his old gig. For cake work at that. Doing something he loved and occasionally answering questions from Nolan, James, or Jordan that had the potential to shaft someone evil, who deserved everything karma could send his way.

Jace had never felt so well rested or invigorated in his whole life. Damn it, he was...happy.

Even if he knew better.

This wasn't going to last forever. Learning from an expert in the field he would sell his left nut to be part of for the rest of his life, who also turned out to be a seriously awesome guy, was lucky enough.

Hanging out with their personal bodyguard who was as easy to talk to as he was to look at was a hell of a bonus. Especially when the same guy took damn good care of Laurel so Jace could concentrate on music.

Nolan accompanied her on her shifts at Devra and Morgan's diner, where they apparently had grown even closer. Jace caught the looks they passed each other when they all gathered around to eat leftovers from the restaurant for dinner and he couldn't deny that he'd shared a few of them with Nolan himself.

They passed the time they weren't working geeking out over the stash of board games they'd discovered inside the weathered trunk that doubled as a coffee table. And when Laurel and Nolan had busted Jace trying to cheat the night before, they'd dissolved into a pillow fight and tickle fest that had nearly led to an entirely different form of entertainment.

Winded, laughing, and completely at ease, they'd collapsed into a tangle on the thick rug on the living room floor in front of the fire. Jace admitted to himself he'd been disappointed when Nolan roused him and carried Laurel to their bed.

He would have gladly traded a crick in his neck today for spending the night with the three of them camped out together. It was dangerous territory, flirting with the invisible boundaries he'd always maintained with Laurel and was now erecting between them and Nolan, too. Damn, he couldn't risk letting their attraction compromise the extra layer of security Nolan provided for Laurel.

Not because she was incapable of looking after herself, but because Jace felt better knowing someone else had her back while she was out of his sight. Otherwise, he'd ask her to stay, and she would even if it meant she was bored out of her mind while he was ignoring her all day. At least until she began to resent him for it.

Despite the chemistry the three of them had oozing between them, Nolan always showed Laurel the respect she deserved, never once trying to peep on her getting changed or taking advantage of his authority. No bullshit like that.

It was full of so much win, he'd be a fool to jeopardize any part of their current arrangements. They were padding their bank accounts with the overly generous fee Jordan paid them in addition to providing free room and board even while they double-dipped with other jobs. Session musician work had never been on his radar, but now that he had a taste of it, he loved it. Meanwhile, Laurel had quickly become Middletown's favorite server in addition to giving Devra and Morgan the suggestions she'd tried to implement at the pub they'd worked at, although their boss hadn't been interested in change. The women had been so impressed with her work ethic and the improvements she'd made that they'd insisted on putting her on their payroll as a consultant in addition to a waitress. She'd also started to talk to Tom and Ms. Brown, the unofficial heads of their ever-expanding Middletown family about her dream of someday helping people through social work.

Tom had hooked them up with the opportunity to volunteer at the shelter in town and Laurel, Jace, and Nolan had all put in some time giving back where they could. He admitted, the warm, fuzzy feeling it gave him was almost as addicting as the rush he got from performing.

Truth was, Laurel no longer had to work at all if she

didn't want to, but Jace suspected she craved being around the other women, who had quickly become friends in addition to employers or clients at the shelter. They were open-minded, unconventional, and accepting...there wasn't a lot not to like.

Yeah. Jace could hardly believe he wasn't living one of the fantasies he'd cooked up while lugging tubs of gross dishes up and down the stairs of the O'Flannery's, where they'd worked after escaping Heels. It was a lot to process, and too good to get used to. Because if it all disappeared again as quickly as it had revolutionized their lives, he wasn't sure he could survive the disappointment.

Jace stretched then hit the bathroom, scrubbing his hand over his face as he turned into the open area of the trendy tiny house he already felt so damn at home in. It was a combo kitchen living room. Barely bigger than the entryway of Jordan's place, it was more than he'd ever dreamed of for himself and Laurel. It was private without any neighbors to argue through definitely-not-up-to-code walls in the middle of the night. Clean, without even a single roach for poor Dottie Long-Tongue to make into a midnight snack.

He reminded himself a million times a day that similar to Nolan's gorgeous guitar, which he'd caved and played a couple of times lately with Kason before returning it to its velvet-lined nest, none of this was actually theirs. They were only borrowing this life as long as they remained useful to the Shields.

Maybe it would be for the best if Draven never got caught.

Jace's stomach cramped at that. Who the hell was he turning into if he only cared about pampering himself at the expense of those still suffering? That was not who he wanted to turn into. No, no way. Fuck.

He trudged into the kitchen, annoyed with himself on a number of levels. Not the least of which was frustration over his raging libido. He'd never had so much trouble controlling his desire before. Being locked up with Nolan and Laurel for large swaths of each day made it impossible to school his dick to stay dormant, especially without the outlet of his usual hookups. He groaned, then hit the brew button on the coffeepot. While it began to spit out his first steaming cup—which would hopefully clear the bullshit from his brain—he braced his hands on the counter, hanging his head.

"You sleep okay?" The baritone of Nolan's voice caressed his ears, nearly as sweet as the music he'd been making with Kason lately.

Jace adjusted his sweatpants in case the last bit of his morning wood decided to regrow in honor of the sexy bastard who'd scooted the coffee table aside to do one-handed pushups while barely breaking a sweat.

"Yeah, man." Jace grabbed his mug, which belonged to a matching set with not a single chip among them, and slouched on the couch, propping his trusty guitar across his lap for extra insurance. Probably wise considering the impressive, well-muscled body demonstrating all it was capable of in front of him. He'd have to take the guy up on working out together more often. Damn.

Even Laurel wasn't immune to Nolan. Jace caught her staring more times than he cared to admit. Frankly, Nolan-watching was a hell of a lot better than streaming trash on the TV the guy blocked with his bulky frame. Jace wondered what it would feel like to fuck a man like that...or be fucked by one.

He strummed his guitar idly. It was beat to hell, had been through a lot, like Jace himself, but it had been high quality once. Nothing like Nolan's or the seemingly endless assortment of instruments Kason brought with him. However, it meant more to Jace. He'd found it in a pawnshop and Laurel had insisted on rescuing it when he'd refused to splurge. It might not be pristine, but it was special to him because of the sacrifice they'd made to own it and what a luxury it had been at the time.

It had been the first time they'd allowed themselves to believe the future could be different. Better than what they'd been living for so long.

Of course, the purchase had paid itself back many times over, especially since he'd been working for Kason, but that had been far from guaranteed.

"Don't you think you're buff enough already?" Jace sniped when Nolan flipped around to his back to start in on his zillion crunch quota for the day.

"Does that mean you do?" Nolan grinned at him, never breaking his pace. "Thanks."

"You're making me look bad."

"To who? Laurel?" Nolan's laugh puffed out as he constricted his perfect fucking abs. "I don't think so. She adores you...and she's totally into that street scrapper vibe you've got going on. I think I'm too much of a pretty boy to be any competition."

Even while exercising, his hair was pretty damn perfect. That bastard.

"It's not like that between us, you know." Jace stared at the bridge of his guitar, fingering chords to a sad song he loved.

Nolan did stop then, sitting up and facing Jace from the floor. "Could be if you wanted it to be. You know that, don't you? Hell, you two already act like you've been married for twenty years. It's...nice."

Jace's gaze swung to Nolan's. Could the guy actually be envious of Jace? What the fuck?

When he paused to think about it, he nodded. "Laurel's been my partner in life, there's no doubt about that. I would never have made it without her. And that's why I'd never risk ruining our friendship with sex. I don't even know if she'd be into it. With me or anyone else."

Jace was sure that aside from a few times it had been fuck or starve after they'd first escaped, she hadn't slept with anyone. She'd told him so enough times for him to be sure she wasn't shitting him. Laurel didn't do casual. And that was fine with him.

"Only one way to find out, really." Nolan shrugged one lightly glistening shoulder.

"Are you saying you want to try?" Jace's hackles rose, but it wasn't fair to go junkyard dog when he wasn't planning on making a move, was it? Just because he wished things were different, didn't mean he had the right to keep Laurel from finding happiness or pleasure with someone else—maybe Nolan—if that's what she wanted.

"Chill out, Jace." Nolan winced. "Grip that thing any harder and you're going to snap its neck."

Jace instantly relaxed his fingers, silently apologizing to his guitar.

"I wasn't trying to creep in on your territory. Just saying, after spending so much time with you two, it's impossible not to notice..." Nolan started doing crunches again, as if he needed to blow off some kind of energy too. "Never mind. None of my business."

Damn straight it wasn't. And that might have been the end of their discussion if Jace's brand new Shields-provided phone—one Jordan had insisted they each carry for safety reasons that neither of them could argue with—hadn't chosen that exact moment to go traitor. The hookup app he'd downloaded out of desperation and curiosity the night before, before taking things into his own hands in the shower, bleeped in a very distinct notification.

The expression that spread slowly over Nolan's face was half-smirk and half-grin. "Discovered the joys of modern technology, have you? Hate to be a cock-blocker, but there's no way in hell I'm letting you out of my sight long enough to screw a stranger."

He shrugged. "Watch if you want. Beats hanging out in the alley behind bars or the bathroom of a club waiting for a random quickie. I mean, at least I assume it would."

Nolan didn't avert his gaze before Jace registered the flare of his pupils. His bodyguard didn't hate that idea. If that's what it took to get off, maybe he'd have to corrupt their goody-two shoes vigilante into escorting him somewhere discreet soon. Hell, maybe Nolan could use a BJ too. What guy couldn't? Jace wouldn't mind sharing a willing hottie with the dude.

Thank god for his guitar. One of the dainty throw pillows wouldn't have hidden the full blown bulge in his sweats.

Nolan grunted. "It's been a long couple of weeks cooped up here, huh?"

"You could say that." They only had one bathroom between the three of them, and sharing a room with Laurel...well, that always riled him up. With Nolan stretched out on the other side of the wall, and only quick jerkoff sessions to relieve the unrelenting pressure, well, it was probably lucky Jace hadn't put someone's eye out by now.

"Come on, let's see who matched with you. Maybe she's hot." Nolan snagged the phone from the coffee table before Jace could react, then swiped it open.

"Hey, how'd you know my passcode?" Jace growled. And, uh, she? Uh oh. Maybe he'd been reading the situation wrong all along.

"I fucking do this for a living. Covert operative, remember? I see you enter it a hundred times a day." Nolan grinned and Jace found it hard to be irritated with him. The guy could be an asshole, sure. But he was fun to be around. As much as Jace wanted to hate Nolan every time Laurel let her guard down a little more around him, he really couldn't bring himself to do it.

Jace had been in the midst of horrible human beings before, enough to know that Nolan wasn't one of them. He was a decent guy, even if he had dumbass moments. Like this one.

"Oh. Shit, sorry. I shouldn't have done that." Nolan popped to his feet. He actually seemed off balance for the first time since Jace had known him.

Jace eyed the phone screen plastered with abs nearly as fine as Nolan's as the guy passed it back to him and evaded Jace's penetrating stare. Enough already. Jace snipped. "What the fuck? You weren't one bit ruffled when we tied you up and took you hostage, but you can't handle seeing a smoking hot dude on my phone? I like men. I fuck them, too. Is that a problem?"

Jace stood up and came nearly face-to-face with Nolan. He was tall as fuck. Jace couldn't say why he was antagonizing him, maybe because he was pissed that he was attracted to Nolan and had thought, just maybe, it wasn't a one-sided admiration. He was damn tired of lusting after people he couldn't have and who didn't want him back.

"Calm down, Jace. I'm not a bigot." Nolan groaned. "I just thought... Because of the way you look at Laurel..."

"Yeah, so?" He didn't have to explain himself to anyone, never mind this person who was being paid to stay with them. Jace better not forget it was Nolan's job to hang, not his pleasure. But somehow, he wished he could. He *liked* Nolan. Having a guy friend was a first, and a perk he'd sort of hoped didn't have to end after this assignment.

But maybe he'd had it all wrong.

"I'm confused and don't want to make assumptions since I'm clearly doing a bad job of it." Nolan held out his hands. "Sorry."

"I'm bisexual," Jace said simply.

At least Nolan didn't leave Jace's declaration hanging awkwardly between them. He rushed to say, "Me too."

"Seriously?" Jace's jaw was the one hanging open then. "'Cause I've seen the way *you* look at Laurel and I assumed..."

Nolan took a step back, out of Jace's reach, then admitted, "Do you blame me? She's stunning. And so full of strength and kindness despite everything that's happened to her it turns me on...I can't explain it. From the first second, outside of Heels, it was like I felt her there before I saw her. I know it's rude, but I can't help staring at her. Uh...but unless you're blind, you'd know that I'm an equal opportunity ogler."

Jace's gaze flew to Nolan's. "Me? You've been watching me?"

"How could you not know?" Nolan stared at the

ceiling. "I mean, I'm good. Used to being covert. Hiding my reactions. But damn, you're oblivious sometimes."

"Maybe I was too busy being jealous." Jace couldn't help one corner of his mouth from tipping up. "And it's not like I have a whole lot of experience with normal relationships. Usually—"

He raised his phone gesturing at the hookup offer accompanied by a glorious dick pic.

"Is Laurel okay with that?" Nolan wondered, though he looked like he'd like to suck the question back in as soon as he'd blurted it out.

"We don't exactly discuss it." Jace shrugged, though he felt like shit every time he gave in and came inside someone else. "Maybe she doesn't know."

"Oh, she knows." Nolan shot Jace a look that said he was being stupid. "You must come home smelling like dive bars and sweaty sex."

"I guess. Probably." Jace speared his hands into his hair. "She's never said anything about it. And besides, I told you it's not like that between us."

"But you wish it was."

Well, shit. He couldn't argue about that.

"I hate to break it to you, bro. The two of you, whether you have sex or not, are wed in the strictest sense of the word. You love each other. You do everything that soulmates do together—dream, make a life, survive every ordinary day. You're partners. So I'm going to say this... I totally get that I am not an expert on the impact your pasts must have had on you, but Jordan pushes mental health hard on our team. Counseling is available to all of us as part of our benefits. Now that you're in a position to get some help, I would ask Kennedy about setting up therapy sessions so you can get this worked out before you fuck up the best thing in both of your lives."

Jace hated that Nolan was right so much that his survival instincts kicked in. He did what he did best and distracted himself from something that was too painful to consider, even if it meant he was shooting himself in the foot in the process. Dysfunction at its finest.

"And if I like raw, emotionless, consensual sex with hot men on the side?" Jace advanced on Nolan, shocked and a little thrilled when the big guy retreated a step and then another until the refrigerator stopped his backward progress in the small space.

He leaned in, smelling the faint sheen of sweat on Nolan's neck before licking a line up it. His hands landed on Nolan's pecs and he kneaded the muscles there. Jace knew a hell of a lot about turning guys on and how to please them. He employed every single bit of that knowledge when he seduced Nolan.

His fingertips glided down, down over their bodyguard's ripped abs then along his sides until Jace slipped them into the waistband of Nolan's shorts.

"Ah, fuck. I guess it's not my place to tell you what you should do." Nolan's stare drilled into Jace's as Jace fished for his cock. It was every bit as thick as these hellish exercise shorts had been promising for weeks now.

Jace wrapped his fist around it and hummed, using it as a handle to keep Nolan in place as he rose onto his tiptoes and crushed his lips to Nolan's parted mouth.

He might have been the aggressor, but Nolan was eager to encourage him. His hips ground against Jace's fist, thrusting his hard-on through Jace's greedy fingers. Jace pinned Nolan to the refrigerator, his own erection rubbing against Nolan's ripped thigh as he began to hump Nolan's leg.

They made out, lashing each other's tongues and swallowing each other's moans and curses as they devoured each other. It seemed like Jace wasn't the only one being driven to distraction by his two sexy roommates. As if having one off-limits gorgeous woman wasn't enough, for the past couple of weeks he'd had two living, breathing temptations around every minute of the day.

And he was taking out every bit of that pent-up frustration on Nolan, his thick lips, and his fat cock. He stroked Nolan as they ground together, his hand trapped between their undulating bodies. It probably wouldn't have been much longer before they were wrestling to see which one of them would end up bent over the stool at the kitchen counter if Laurel hadn't stumbled from their room, rubbing her bleary eyes right then.

Was it because she was still half-asleep or because she couldn't believe what she was seeing?

She froze but didn't turn around, and certainly didn't stop staring at the two men, locked in a very intimate and undeniable embrace that was *exactly* what it looked like.

Jace withdrew his hand from Nolan's pants, though neither of their hard-ons were going to be difficult to spot. He wrenched away from Nolan, but was breathing so heavily he couldn't even gasp out an excuse of some sort.

"Oh damn. I'm sorry." Laurel slapped a hand over her eyes, then scurried past them toward the door while still in her thin cotton pajamas. It was a testament to how fucked up they were by desire and lack of blood flow to the brain that neither of them stopped her.

"I'll give you two some space. Don't worry, I'll go next

door to Devra's or Hot Rides if she's not there. Uh, enjoy." Laurel kept her eyes on the ground as she snagged her coat off a hook by the door and stuffed her bare feet into the new boots the Powertools ladies had included in the bags of donated clothes they'd hooked her up with.

Before Jace could reset his brain, which was still short-circuited by lust, she had slipped out the door.

"Well, fuck." Nolan rearranged his dick and balls, which were probably nearly as sore as Jace's.

At least his boner wasn't an issue anymore. His cock had deflated at the sight of Laurel fleeing and the dread that followed. One stupid move might have destroyed their relationship. "I did exactly what you were warning me not to do, didn't I?"

"I'll fix this." Nolan stepped closer and kissed Jace again, this time with tenderness and caring that did more to rock Jace's world than their passion had. Especially since it felt like a kiss goodbye.

"It's not your fault."

"Didn't say it was, not entirely. But I think I can talk you out of it better than you can. Go get your head on straight and I'll bring your girl back in a bit. Think about what you really want long-term, and if she gives you another chance, don't fuck that one up."

It was more than Jace deserved. The cramp in his chest made it obvious that Nolan wasn't too far off the mark. The thought of losing Laurel had the power to wreck him. He couldn't let that happen. Maybe it was time to come clean with her. "Thanks, man."

Nolan nodded, then flashed his lopsided grin. "It's going to be okay. I'll make sure of it."

Jace slogged into their room to mull things over while

Nolan raced out into the cold after Laurel, still wearing only his paper thin shorts.

He'd be fine. If there was one thing Jace had no doubt about, it was that the man was hot as fucking hell. Jace, on the other hand, was screwed.

10

————

"How fucking stupid are you?" Nolan grumbled at himself. He welcomed the shock of the late winter air slapping him in his flushed cheeks, wrapping in icy tendrils around his pounding heart, and shrinking his package. As if messing around with two people with more baggage than an entire airport wasn't dumb enough, they were clients, informants, and people he should be concentrating on keeping safe.

Worst of all, he would never forgive himself if he caused a rift between Laurel and Jace when they so obviously loved and needed each other. "Damn it!"

He spotted the swish of Laurel's chestnut hair and the pure white of her faux-fur lined coat right before she disappeared into the neighboring house where Devra, Trevon, and Quinn—who also happened to be the manager at Hot Rides—lived.

Just what he needed, witnesses to his moronic life decisions. Especially since in their tight-knit community, of which Jordan was part, there no way his boss wouldn't find out about the lines Nolan had crossed. At the speed news traveled around here, Nolan might only have seconds before he was ratted out. It might be fucked up, but he loved what he did for a living. Maybe not the methods they had to use to make the world slightly less shitty, but the end result. And he didn't think putting assassin on his resume would get him very many callbacks.

Okay, true, with how much he got paid he probably didn't have to do anything else once he was done with Shields, but he would have hunted down these assholes for free.

Ignoring the pebbles that bit his bare feet, he sprinted after Laurel and banged on Devra's door.

"No need to break it down." The woman—with waist-length inky hair, eyes rimmed with artful dark liner, and burgundy lips that complimented her Middle Eastern complexion—answered with a shake of her head that set the gold jewelry she preferred swinging and tinkling around her.

"Sorry." Nolan tried to get himself under control. It was nearly impossible with the memory of Jace's cock imprinted on his abs and his lips still puffy from the other man's aggressive, and *very* welcome, kiss. Not to mention the equally extreme though opposite reaction he was having to the possibility of hurting Laurel. He might not have been as controlled as Aarav, but it wasn't often he found himself in a tornado of emotions.

He took a deep breath and pretended he was on a mission, in that moment right before preparation descended into the madness of deadly action.

"You okay?" Devra asked, stepping back to let him in. There weren't many options on where to go in the tight quarters so he ended up standing beside Laurel, though they didn't make eye contact.

Nolan wasn't sure which of them Devra was addressing. She looked at them both, a perfectly painted on brow arched as she scanned each of them, flushed cheeks and all.

"Yeah, of course." Laurel's smile didn't reach her eyes, which still refused to meet his gaze. Of course, that meant she was studying his naked torso and the red marks Jace's fingers had left on his shoulders and pecs.

Oops.

"Okay, well..." Devra patted Nolan's bare abs. "I need to run some food over to the mechanics at the shop. It's past their usual break time. Why don't you two hash out whatever is obviously going on between you in private? But fair warning...it took me longer than I'd planned to finish because I was making extras. Heard they have some guests and they're probably going to be headed this way after they load up on lunch."

"Who?" Nolan narrowed his eyes.

"Sola, Kennedy, and Devon stopped by the garage to talk to Wren. You know they're not going to be able to resist checking in on you guys. Hell, they probably came over mostly for that and are hanging out at Hot Rides first so they don't seem as nosey as they actually are."

Laurel didn't seem too put out by that. Her sister-in-law and the two agents from Shields were quickly becoming her squad. "Great, because I could use a sounding board right about now. A female perspective, if you know what I mean."

"I do. I do." Devra nodded, making her nose ring sparkle. "I'm always willing to listen, too."

"Thanks, I was kind of counting on that." Laurel

sighed. "I'm not used to having people to blab to but, damn it, I kind of like it and I intend to take advantage while I have all of you around."

Devra held her arms out, open, and let Laurel choose if she wanted a hug. Laurel accepted, walking into the other woman's embrace. "My ears are always open and my hugs are free. I guarantee the rest of the ladies at Hot Rides right now would say the same."

Nolan groaned. "They're going to make my life miserable."

"You seem to be doing a good enough job of that on your own, mister." Devra squeezed his hand to soften the censure in her words. "But if you're worried, why don't you try to fix whatever you've done before they descend on this place?"

Nolan cut his gaze to Laurel's. "I plan to."

Devra nodded, hefted her tray of food from the kitchen counter, and headed for the door. Nolan opened it for her. "Do you need help with that?"

"I think you have more important things to worry about." She winked. "I'm fine. Thanks, though."

Nolan shut the door gently after her, then took a deep breath or three before turning around and resting his shoulders on it. "I'm sorry, Laurel. I was really out of line. That was totally unprofessional of me. I have no idea what I was thinking."

"You were thinking that Jace is fucking hot and you'd like to kiss him. Or more." Laurel sighed. "Besides, it looked like he was the one going after you, not the other way around. I don't blame you one damn bit for giving in. If he ever kissed me like that, I'd forget how to think straight too."

"He wasn't doing anything I haven't imagined a

thousand times since I met you two." Nolan grimaced, letting Jace off the hook. The truth was, he'd baited the guy, teasing him about the hook up app when the air had already been so charged between them.

"Was it as good as you thought?" Laurel wondered.

"I'm not sure what you want me to say. Yes, so you know what you've been missing out on. Or no, so you think I'm not as into him as it seemed and you can pretend it wouldn't rock your world if you two ever actually tried it yourselves." Nolan shrugged.

"Say no. Definitely no." Laurel's response rushed out as if in desperation.

"That would be a lie."

"*Now* you're afraid to break the rules?" She threw up her hands and made a growl of frustration that did nothing to tamp down the desire simmering inside him. "Help a girl out, would you?"

"I'd like to. Except that would be repeating the same mistake." Nolan itched to reach for her, but it would only dig them in deeper. Though, as she'd pointed out... sometimes doing the wrong thing felt awfully damn right.

"Wait...what?" Laurel looked up at him then, her brows knitted together. "I want Jace to be happy, and if that means having you, well, you heard Devra. I can always find something to keep me occupied and out of your way for a while. Don't worry about me."

"Come on. I'm not Jace. I don't silently tolerate shit very well and denial is not my forte. You have to know I'm as attracted to you as I am to him and it's frustrating the hell out of me to watch you two dance around each other when you'd be so damn good together." There. He'd admitted it. "Jace is afraid to hurt you by taking something he thinks you're not ready or willing to give, and you're convinced he's not into you because he has the control of a goddamned saint. Clearly more than I have, anyway. I cracked after less than a month of being bombarded by the sexual tension that's flying between you two constantly. Never mind all the years you two have been stuck in this cycle of perpetual foreplay and denial. Living in that tiny house with the two of you is like being caught in a whirlwind of desire, and I'm not the kind of man who sits on his hands when there's a solution—or a sexy partner, or two—within reach. I get that sex probably means something a lot different to me than it does to you two. Between consenting adults, it's fun and natural and hard for me to think of reasons why I shouldn't indulge whenever and with whomever I feel like getting off with. It's the relationship part you and Jace nailed that I've never really had a chance, or the desire, to try before. I'm jealous as fuck."

"Oh." Laurel blinked a few times.

"That doesn't freak you out, does it?" Nolan scrubbed his hand over his face. "I'll ask Jordan to assign someone else to your case if it does. I'm sure Sola would be more than happy—"

"Don't go. Don't leave us." Laurel stepped closer and put her fingers on his wrist, pressing until he lowered it and she could peer up into his eyes from closer than she ever had before. "Unless it's too much for you to deal with. I'm well aware of the toll it can take on your soul to want something and never have it. To sacrifice so the person you're obsessed with doesn't have to deal with your bullshit."

Nolan reached out but stopped short of touching Laurel until she leaned into his caress. He stroked her hair as he murmured, "That's probably the definition of love, you know. Wanting someone else to be happy even if it's at your expense. But it doesn't make it healthy."

"Which is why I don't blame you for making out with Jace. It's not your fault. He doesn't even realize how hot he is. Ugh." Laurel rolled her eyes.

"Oh hell yes, he does." Nolan remembered the fierce intensity in Jace's gaze as he'd stalked Nolan through the kitchen. "Don't be fooled. He's hiding an awful lot of himself from you because he thinks it makes you safer."

"What if he's right?" Laurel bit her lower lip.

"He would never hurt you. You must know that." Nolan tipped his head.

"Of course. Not on purpose." She sighed. "There are parts of Jace no one else sees. You two are nothing alike. You're gentle and sweet and bright light."

Nolan tried not to laugh as he mentally tallied his body count.

"Jace is dark and fierce but loyal. And somehow I'm drawn to you both. I do worry that if Jace and I ever crossed that line, maybe one of us—or both of us— wouldn't be able to handle it when he really lets loose. And at the same time, I'm afraid I could never trust anyone else as much as I trust him, so I've never even... you know."

Nolan couldn't believe she thought her roommate was the more sinister of the two of them given what he did for a living. He probably would have said so if she hadn't shocked him first. "Are you saying you haven't been with anyone at all since you left Draven?"

She swallowed hard then nodded. "I mean, not for fun. There were a couple of times it was that or Jace and I weren't going to eat for a week. I don't care about myself, but I couldn't sit there and watch him starve."

And damn if that didn't trigger every bit of his nature. For the same reasons he'd baited Jace, Nolan wished he could encourage Laurel to get over her fears and take what she deserved. But he knew it wasn't that simple. Not for her. "After all this time I imagine willingly sharing that with a partner you care for has been built up into something major in your mind."

"Exactly. Of course you get it." Laurel chewed her index finger then whispered, "Feel free to say no, but if I wanted to break the ice...would you volunteer to help me out?"

Nolan grinned and stayed glued to the floor but he shifted so that his arms were open to her. It made his entire year when a mischievous smile curled Laurel's rosy lips and she took a step closer. "I mean, it would serve Jace right...wouldn't it?"

"I'm willing to be a pawn in your game." Nolan shrugged.

"Maybe I could have what he did. A taste. A kiss." Laurel went up on her tiptoes and laid her palms on his bare chest, tempting Nolan to howl. His cock roared back to life and begged him to remind her that Jace's hand had been down his pants too. Not that he would. He'd gladly accept anything she decided to share with him and prize it, knowing what it meant to her—and him—because of that.

In fact, he stood there, stone still as she advanced on him, not nearly as aggressively as her roommate had but every bit as seductively. Laurel stared up at him with wide, gorgeous hazel eyes, then laid her lips on his and gently swiped them across his parted mouth.

He didn't hesitate then, refusing to let her think for an instant that he thought she was damaged goods, like she'd feared Jace might. He showed her with silky caresses and tender sighs precisely how much he loved it when she let herself be vulnerable and he did the same in return.

Her arms went around his neck and her fingers speared into his hair. It said an awful lot that he didn't even mind when she mussed it. Instead he groaned and slipped his tongue out to dart across hers.

As he held her in his arms and she melted against him, he started to dream. What if Jace was there behind him and they had a shot at a real relationship like the one James shared with his spouses or Jordan with his or Devra with her two men? Was it too much to hope for that he could find not only one but two partners who perfectly balanced him out?

Probably.

Especially when there was no damn privacy to be had. He heard the din of chattering voices only a moment before the door was flung open and a cold breeze rushed inside, washing over him and Laurel. He spun, sheltering her flushed face and rapid, shallow breathing from whoever was busting in on them.

"Nolan, where the hell are the rest of your clothes? It's freezing out there," Sola asked with payback glinting in her eye. He instantly regretted those times he'd ribbed her about Aarav's crush on her. Turnabout aimed at him was one thing. But Laurel...

Knowing she hadn't chosen to kiss anyone but him in years, maybe ever, spurred his protective tendencies.

"Left them over at the other house. I better go get them. Come on, Laurel." He reached for her hand, but she didn't take it. When he spun around, her eyes were glassy and unfocused. *Shit!* "Laurel! Are you okay?"

She snapped out of wherever she'd gone, blinking as

she scanned the room. She touched her lips and smiled faintly at him before shrinking from Sola's concerned gaze. Right behind her, Kennedy, Devra, and Devon piled into the tiny home.

Fuck their timing.

"I'll take you home." Nolan wrapped his arm around her shoulders and prepared to lead her through the throng of curious ladies like a starlet through a sea of paparazzi, but she shook her head.

"Would you mind if we didn't rush right back into the fire?" She sighed, wormed out from beneath his biceps, then sank onto Devra's couch. "I think I need a minute to decompress. Things are changing so fast. I'm getting dizzy."

Kennedy glared at Nolan, then rushed to Laurel's side. She murmured something to Laurel, who nodded, before she placed her fingers on Laurel's wrist, measuring her pulse.

Nolan could have already told the doctor that it would be racing. Hell, his was too.

11

———

Laurel stared at the intersection of her wrist and Kennedy's slender fingers. How could someone so young be a doctor? Her excitement dampened as she remembered how much of her life had been wasted, out of her control.

She peeked up at Nolan then. He was absolutely right. She'd spent too long stuck in a platonic rut with Jace, simply because it was comfortable and safe. But was she ready to take a risk if it meant she might lose him entirely? And what the hell was she supposed to do about the fact that she suddenly found herself with a crush on not one but two of her roomies, who apparently had a thing for each other too?

Laurel groaned. Why couldn't life ever be simple?

"Are you okay?" Kennedy asked kindly, her pale blue eyes evaluating each and every clench of Laurel's jaw.

"Yes, thanks." Laurel smiled and gently took her arm back. It was new and a little intimidating to have so many people concerned about her wellbeing. Sometimes it could feel invasive, though she knew they didn't mean it to be. Especially when, at that very moment, she was already doing so much better than she'd ever been before in her lifetime.

Her sister-in-law edged nearer. "Do you want me to call James to come spend some time with you? I'm not sure what's going on, but it seems like you could use someone in your corner."

Devon glared at Nolan. She might have been the smallest of the women gathered around, but she was intense. She and Devra stood shoulder to shoulder. The contrast between their blond and black hair was dramatic, and yet each of them was gorgeous. They were made of the same stuff—dignity, power, and self-assuredness.

Laurel hoped one day she could be more like them. Wren too. Jordan's wife, much taller than her friends, peeked over their shoulders, then scowled at Nolan too.

"Why do you all assume I did something stupid?" He shrugged.

Laurel couldn't help it—she laughed. "To be fair, Jace started it."

"See." Nolan winked at her and she thought, maybe for the first time in forever, that everything was going to be okay. This could be her future, if she adapted and allowed herself to grow. Nolan had been right about that.

"Well, that I believe." Kennedy shook her head, setting her wavy platinum hair dancing around her. "He has the look of a troublemaker. An awfully sexy one, mind you, but a heartbreaker for sure."

"Don't let Marcus hear you talking like that." Sola nudged her co-worker with her elbow and Kennedy groaned.

"Do *not* start acting like Nolan, please. One of him is enough on our team."

Nolan scooched closer to Sola, probably to take the heat off himself. "You know, she has a point. Why is it that Marcus always ends up covering your ass on missions, huh?"

"We work well together." Kennedy shrugged. "That doesn't mean there's anything else going on. I've pretty much sworn off men—they're more trouble than they're worth. I have a vibrator. I can take care of myself without the inevitable disappointment."

Laurel thought she had a point. Maybe with some of their spare cash she should treat herself to a mechanical boyfriend and leave the rest of this stuff alone before she fucked up one of the best things in her life: her partnership with Jace.

Devon cracked up at that. "If you think sex toys can replace a man, or five, who know their way around a woman's body, you've been doing this wrong, friend."

"Well, I'm not about to argue with that. I suck at dating." Kennedy's wry smile brimmed with sadness. "Which is why I certainly wouldn't screw around with someone I entrust my life to regularly. Could you imagine getting in a fight then being distracted in the middle of one of our ops? I wouldn't put myself or any of you in a deadly position like that. Our jobs are a little more dangerous than most, you know?"

"You're right. That sounds like a horrible idea." Why did Sola seem bummed at the revelation? Maybe she was more into Aarav than she was letting on. Whew. Laurel hated to think it, but she was glad she wasn't the only one around there with issues. It made her feel less broken, and...oddly...more normal. *Huh.*

These people were so open and made her comfortable. Before she realized it, she said, "I hear you about swearing off guys. I did the same. I haven't been with anyone, well, ever, really. You know in a consenting relationship anyway, and now I'm stuck day and night with both Jace and Nolan being all..."

Laurel waved her hands at Nolan's ripped abs and that alluring V that vanished beneath the waistband of his shorts. She didn't blame Jace for dipping his hand inside and copping a feel of the prominent bulge the thin cotton couldn't disguise when he was working out, which he spent a significant portion of each day doing.

"I could see where that could get frustrating." Devra grinned. "Believe it or not, you and I have some things in common. Did you know Trevon and I were married before we met Quinn, but we, uh, didn't consummate our vows until after he came into the picture?"

"Seriously?" Laurel leaned forward. "You three seem so perfect together, and Trevon adores you."

"Sometimes it takes the right combination to unlock the bullshit we're carrying around that's holding us back. And no one would blame you at all for having more than the usual share of that." Devra smiled kindly.

Which reminded Laurel... She looked to Kennedy. "Nolan mentioned that there's counseling available through the Shields for agents and informants."

She cleared her throat, wondering if it had been a mistake to ask for help, but Kennedy bridged what could have been an awkward gap and drew out her phone without question.

"Girl, yeah. I put info about it in the pile of papers that went into your onboarding packet. I should have circled back to make sure you'd read through it. I'm sending you a link to the mental health site right now. Your username and password are in the behavioral health folder. Dig it up, log in, read the therapists' bios and pick someone you think could help. You can set up a meeting to get to know them, and if it's a good fit, Jordan's insurance will take care of the rest. Anything you need, we'll make sure you have it." Kennedy looked up at Wren, who smiled sadly.

"Jordan and I lost someone very special to us. It wrecked us for a long time and we only recently found each other again." Wren lowered her voice. "Learn from our mistakes. Get help and work through your issues, so you can figure out what you really want before you miss out on what could be the best thing in your life."

"Are you implying I should hook up with Jace?"

"Fuck yes." Devon was first to say it, but the rest of the women nodded. "It's obvious you two belong together."

"What if he's not the only guy I'm interested in?" Laurel scanned the room waiting to see what the women's reaction would be. All of them were grinning and Nolan looked like he might pass out from holding his breath.

"If you're expecting one of us to tell you that it's wrong to want two men for yourself, you'll be waiting until your pussy dries up and falls off. Go ahead, be a greedy bitch." Devon didn't mess around. Laurel could see why James adored her. "I never imagined this is how my life would turn out, but being spoiled by my two guys and the rest of their friends—not only in bed but through all of life's ups and downs—yeah, it's the best thing I have going."

Laurel snorted at Devon's irreverence, but she was touched too. Something in her unfurled, and she peeked at Nolan's reaction out of the corner of her eye.

He held his hand out to her. "Maybe we should go check in on Jace?"

It certainly didn't make her like him any less when he

thought of her best friend at least as much as he was considering the ramifications for himself or even her.

"Don't let him off easy," Sola advised. "Insist that he gives you an orgasm, or three, for every day he left you in limbo, wondering if he really cared as much as you hoped. You earned them."

It sounded to her like Aarav's stony unwillingness to admit to the attraction between him and Sola was causing some damage of its own. Laurel decided Nolan, with all his cringe-worthy remarks and good-natured ribbing, had only been trying to help his friends. That also didn't make her like him any less, damn it.

Maybe if Laurel could figure out her own damn sex life, she could team up with Nolan to play matchmaker for the rest of the Shields. Now *that* sounded like fun.

And so did the rest of the afternoon, if they could bring Jace around to this fantasy they must both be dreaming about after the seeds the Powertools, Hot Rides, and Shields ladies had planted in her mind. Could their reality become her life, too?

Suddenly, she wanted to find out. No more stalling.

Laurel shot to her feet and snatched Nolan's hand. She tugged him toward the door, or tried, anyway. At the last second he hesitated, looking back at Wren, which jolted her to a halt.

"Hurry up before I chicken out," she hissed at him.

"Will Jordan care? I mean, I'm willing to lose my job over this...but I hope I won't have to." Nolan confided in his boss's wife.

Laurel sucked in a breath. She hadn't even considered the possible ramifications for him.

Wren grimaced. "I'll talk to him. I can't make you any promises, but he knows what it's like to be where you are and clearly, you're the kind of man who will only do what Laurel and Jace want. He asked you to take care of them, and I don't think anyone could argue that you're not."

Laurel nodded. "I think we needed you to make this happen. So...if it's not going to ruin your life...can we get on with it?"

"How about this?" Sola volunteered. "I'll cover you guys. Go take care of whatever you need to, off the clock. I'll check in with James and let him know I'm staying to keep an eye on the place until you tell me you're ready to go back on shift. Take your time. I was planning on hanging out here for the rest of the day anyway."

Nolan extended his arm, his palm perpendicular to the floor. "I owe you."

"Big time." Sola hopped to high-five him with a resounding crack. "Now get the hell out of here."

Laurel felt giddy, and also slightly sick, as her fingers entwined with Nolan's and they jogged back to the house they shared and the man waiting for them both inside.

12

Through the window, Laurel could see Jace pacing like a caged animal. She remembered the sleepless nights he'd practically worn a path in the stained carpet of Draven's hovel, where they'd been kept. Seeing him reduced to old habits made her guts clench.

This wasn't a game, not for either of them.

"Go ahead," Nolan encouraged her, nudging her toward the door. "I'll follow your lead. Whatever happens, I'm okay with it as long as the two of you are."

"What if he freaks out?" Laurel stared at her pretty new boots on the cheery welcome mat.

"I'll be there," Nolan promised. "I'll help defuse the situation. Just remember how much you two love each other and the rest will fade away."

"Okay." She gulped. "But what if *I* freak out?"

"I know you've only just met me. Still, I hope you know that I've got your back. And so does Jace. You're protected here, with us, so take the opportunity and explore while you've got an extra safety net."

The last icy chains of fear burst from around Laurel's heart. She looked up at Nolan and nodded. "Thanks. I want to do this."

"Then let's go." Nolan beamed down at her. He didn't open the door for her, but he was right on her ass when she walked through it.

Jace's head snapped up and he stopped so short he nearly tripped. Before she could utter even a single syllable, he blurted, "I'm sorry. Laurel, shit, I'm *so* sorry. Don't hate me."

"You might want to save that apology for when you actually fuck up." Laurel waved him off. "Besides, if you owe me one, then I owe you one too."

"For what?" Jace narrowed his eyes before flicking his stare to Nolan.

"I kissed him too." Laurel shrugged, half expecting Jace to lunge for Nolan. "And I liked it. A lot."

"Oh." Jace swallowed hard. "Damn, that's worse. I didn't mean to cut in on your...whatever you have going on."

Nolan wisely kept his mouth shut and let her do the talking. He didn't try to defend himself or say he was sorry because they both knew he damn well wasn't and that he'd make out with either of them again if they gave him the slightest opportunity. Laurel loved that he was so direct and honest about his intentions. She didn't have to wonder where she stood with him.

Unlike with Jace, whose contrition was rapidly morphing into some combination of jealousy and irritation. "You know, if you two needed *me* out of the picture, you could have told me so."

Was that hurt in his deep brown eyes? "Jace—"

"I'm sure the Hot Rides gang wouldn't mind if I hung

out at the shop for a few hours." He spoke over her as if he couldn't hear the truth.

"Oh, once things go down, I doubt that's going to be long enough to get it out of our systems." Nolan chuckled and Laurel tapped his rock-solid abs with the back of her hand. Now was not the time. Jace was not in a kidding mood and she wasn't about to risk him taking Nolan seriously.

"For the record, Jace..." Laurel gathered every molecule of bravery she possessed. She stepped close to him, carefully, cautiously, until she could reach out and put her hands on his knotted shoulders. "I would have kissed you every damn day and night of the past ten or twenty years if you'd let me."

"Huh?" Jace gave her his full attention then. His stare locked on hers. This close, there was no denying the effect her confession had on him. His pupils dilated and he held his breath.

"You heard me." She was tired of playing these fucked-up games. Rules they'd invented to keep them safe but not entirely happy.

"I didn't think you were interested in that anymore. With anyone, never mind me." Jace softened a bit, his hands coming up to cup her elbows, his thumbs brushing over the backs of her arms, making her shiver though no part of her was cold. Not while she was the object of both his and Nolan's complete attention.

"Maybe not at first. I was too scared. But over time...if you'd taken that step, been assertive, promised it was okay, and led me there gently, I would have gone with you," Laurel whispered. "You're the only man I trust enough to surrender to."

She looked over her shoulder at Nolan, hoping that

didn't upset him. But it was true. As much as she craved him, she'd never be able to enjoy herself in bed with someone if Jace wasn't there. With him, well, that was a different story. Hopefully Nolan wouldn't mind that she needed another man as a crutch. The truth was, Jace was a part of her, and if Nolan wanted to participate in her awakening, Jace was included in that package.

Somehow she didn't think he would mind. He winked at her.

Jace drew her attention back to him when he blew out a sigh. "I would never have done that. I couldn't. I wouldn't risk scaring you. If you ever looked at me with fear in your eyes, I couldn't take it."

"And that's why you two are in the situation you're in now. And what a lovely pickle it is." Nolan raked Jace with his gaze, lingering on his crotch with a fond smirk. "You were stuck in a rut so deep you needed someone to tow you out. Waiting for each other to break first, it was never going to happen. You two are too noble and stubborn for your own good. Me? Not so much."

He shrugged, though Laurel caught a hint of regret in his eyes. Did he honestly believe he wasn't a decent person? The past few weeks had taught her otherwise. "I hope at least I've fixed that for you."

"Don't think you're off the hook." Laurel shot him a look. "Now that it's out in the open, the magnetism between the three of us is going to be super distracting if we try to ignore it again. We have to live together, in close quarters, for who knows how much longer—probably weeks."

"Months," Nolan corrected. Jace groaned.

Laurel thought about sleeping in his arms or watching movies while pinned between him and Nolan on the barely big enough couch. She was not complaining, but if they didn't do something, she—and likely both of them, too—were going to lose it eventually.

"You're right. The last thing I should be is preoccupied when it comes to your safety." Nolan growled. "We don't expect Draven to come anywhere near here, but I should be as alert as if he was on his way. Fuck. I'm sorry."

He spun and stared out the window, his back heaving as he lashed himself.

"I'm not." Laurel patted Jace's chest, then reached out to Nolan. She put her hand on his shoulder and nudged him until he turned around to face them once more. "What I'm proposing is that we cut the tension the old-fashioned way."

There. She'd said it. But the two handsome-as-hell dolts staring back at her didn't seem to understand what she'd said.

"Huh?" Jace asked again as he tipped his head. It would have been funny if she hadn't been spilling her guts and laying her deepest, most forbidden fantasies out in the open in broad daylight.

"Let's fuck and get it out of our systems." Laurel shrugged. "It's just sex, right?"

Jace stepped closer and put his arms around her. He laid his forehead against hers and murmured, "What is this about? We both know there is no such thing as *just sex* for you."

"Maybe I wish there was." She leaned against him. "Maybe there could be some day. And that's what I'm asking for your help with. Please?"

"You're serious?" Jace cupped her cheeks in his steady hands, tipping her face up toward his so he could read the absolute certainty in her gaze.

"Yeah." She nodded, thinking of Kennedy, Devon, Sola, Wren, and the rest of the strong-ass women she'd met since the Shields had found her. Since they'd been living at Hot Rides and hanging out with her brother and his spouses. She was ready to join their ranks. Become someone who overcame her past and didn't let it steal potential joy from her future.

"And you're sure you want that with both of us?" Nolan asked from over Jace's shoulder as he shifted from foot to foot. "I mean, you two have known each other forever and have something real. I'm happy to bow out..."

"No way. No one's giving anyone space. We're going to do the opposite of that." Laurel reached for him, curling her fingers in the waistband of his shorts and yanking him closer. "There's chemistry here, and Jace should have what he desires too. It's obvious that's you. If I'm going to do this, it's going be my way. I'm dying to be selfish. Spoiled. And I'm only going to feel really great about that if you two enjoy it too. You're both hot as hell. Nolan, you're new and exciting, and Jace is sexy and familiar."

"If you think I haven't drooled over you every single day since I met you, you're not paying attention." Jace drew her attention back to him. "But if you want Nolan too, I'm not going to deny you that or pretend like I won't enjoy the hell out of sharing him with you."

"Here's the truth. There's only been one man in my life who made me feel secure before: Jace." Laurel smiled at him. "And now, suddenly, there are two. Maybe it's that or maybe there's something about this freaky town, but... I finally feel like I can let loose a little. Don't prove me wrong, okay?"

Jace hugged her. "You are safe with us, but that doesn't mean you have to sleep with us."

"I know. But...I want to. And I'm getting the feeling neither of you hate the idea either. So we're going to do this?" Laurel's heart rate shot up. Her fingers twisted in the hem of her sweater and began to lift it.

"Yeah. We are." Jace looked to Nolan, who nodded emphatically.

"But not like that." Jace halted the progress of her clothes over her skin. "If I'm going to indulge after all this time, I intend to savor the moment. Is that okay?"

Laurel bit her lip. It would be harder to pretend this was only about physical release if the guys didn't act like savages who simply claimed her. It was more treacherous than anything they'd talked about so far, but she couldn't help the part of her that itched to see what that kind of intimacy felt like...

So she agreed. "Yeah. Just...hurry."

Nolan chuckled and Jace groaned.

13

J ace surveyed the room. Given the short notice and how unprepared he'd been for Laurel's demands, he figured he and Nolan had done damn fine creating a romantic vibe. Sure, she'd said what they were about to do was only about physical relief, but he couldn't stand the thought of her finally allowing herself to be exposed enough to explore her sexuality and him being unable to show her that intimacy was nothing like what they'd experienced before, even when it wasn't about forever.

Hell, he was pretty much the king of hookups and he'd never once treated his partners with anything but the respect and appreciation they deserved for sharing themselves with him to their mutual satisfaction. What Laurel might not realize is that even "just sex" came with powerful-though-temporary emotions. He had to be absolutely sure anything they did wouldn't contribute to her closing herself off again for another couple of decades.

He hated to admit it, but having Nolan there might be

a brilliant tactic to ensure things stayed fun and friendly. If it took a chaperone to make sure he didn't do anything stupid, like take things too far and drop the L-bomb when he came inside her, he was good with that. Especially when the guy she'd picked to get freaky with was one Jace had been eying for weeks.

Candles flickered around the room, washing it with patchy bronze light. Soft blankets and every pillow in place piled together made sure the bed looked nothing like the dirty bare mattresses or cold, hard floors of their nightmares. Nor did it look like the ultra-fancy places they'd been trapped in when they were younger.

It was cozy, welcoming...casual. The smell of cinnamon—not expensive perfume or unwashed sheets—filled the air. He couldn't believe this was about to go down. What the fuck had his life become? In a matter of weeks they'd gone from scraping their way to middle class to a place where things he'd never imagined possible kept happening.

"You okay?" Laurel asked from the doorway.

"Yeah." He pushed off the dresser he'd been leaning against and ambled over to her, cupping her face in his hands. "Sorry. Thinking about how a couple of weeks have changed everything, absolutely everything, for the better."

Nolan edged up behind her, and Jace could already tell a difference in Laurel because she didn't flinch. She was relaxed between them, unafraid and open.

"I know and I honestly feel greedy because I'm hoping for even more, but this..." Laurel bit her lower lip.

"It's the right time. You're ready. And we're going to be here with you." Jace held his hand out to her and, without hesitation, she set her palm in his. He squeezed her fingers. "Thank you for choosing me."

"And me," Nolan echoed. "If you decide Jace is more than enough for you—"

Laurel snatched his waistband and yanked, drawing them both into the bedroom. Jace chuckled. The thing was, when Laurel made up her mind, there was no stopping her. He knew better than to stand between her and what she went after even if, by some miracle, it was him. And their hot bodyguard.

But first... "There's something I've been dying to do."

"Yeah?" she asked coyly, peeking up at him from beneath her naturally thick, curled lashes.

This time Jace didn't tell himself no, not when she'd already outright requested what he'd dreamed of forever. He wrapped his arm around her waist and used the lush curves of her fine ass to drag her to him. "I can't believe he got to kiss you before I did."

"Oh." Her gaze softened and she reached for him, her arms draping over his shoulders. "I'm sorry. I didn't plan for any of this."

"I know. But you can make it up to me now," he teased. "I've only been waiting like twenty-five years for this moment."

Laurel sighed, then went onto her tiptoes, pressing her mouth to his. He sucked in a hiss, his lips parting, and before he could fully believe he was holding Laurel—his Laurel—and finally tasting that sweet smile, she slipped her tongue into his mouth.

It meant something to him, something major, because that was one thing they'd never done. Not many people dared to try it when they could so easily be bitten. The fact that she went there, with him, right away, meant she put her full faith in him. He swore then and there he would not fuck this up.

Jace groaned, the closeness of Laurel in his arms in a very unplatonic embrace even more satisfying than he'd imagined those millions of times. He speared his fingers into her thick hair and massaged the back of her head, encouraging her to take anything and everything she desired from him as what little chill he had remaining crumbled.

They ate at each other, their movements filled with possession, greed, and very delayed gratification. Underlying their passion was something he'd never experienced before. Bone-deep consideration and, yes, love. Making out with someone he cared so much about took their kiss to a whole new level. It blew his mind as much as it turned him on.

Nolan muttered a curse as he sandwiched Laurel between them, massaging her shoulders and leaning in for an up-close view of Laurel and Jace's first kiss. Jace prayed that he didn't embarrass himself and come on the spot.

The ecstasy that flooded through his veins with every sigh and soft groan Laurel emitted as they made out had the power to overwhelm him. His cock stiffened, already primed by Nolan's so-different lip lock and grope earlier. No one would blame him from being pushed past his limits by these two gorgeous, and decent, people—one of whom he loved and the other who was fresh, hot AF, and so damn exciting.

Jace didn't mean to, but he started walking toward the bed, edging Laurel away from Nolan and up to it. She didn't freak when the back of her knees tapped the side of the mattress. Instead she broke away from him, both of them sighing, his heart about to explode from pounding so hard. She licked her lips, shot him and Nolan a shy smile, then sank into the nest he'd made for them.

Laurel reclined on the bed and watched as he and Nolan stalked closer. When he leaned over her and slid his hand beneath the hem of her shirt, petting her softly rounded belly, she scrunched her eyes closed, then asked, her voice trembling just the slightest bit, "Will you two get naked first?"

Jace knew right then that despite her bravado, Laurel wasn't as confident as she seemed. How many times had she strutted around their apartment with nothing on, teasing him mercilessly? Testing their boundaries and incorrectly assuming he wasn't interested in looking...or more. But suddenly, baring herself made her nervous. *Huh.*

He didn't hesitate and neither did Nolan. It was tough to say whose clothes hit the floor first, but when Jace looked over, the other guy's broad shoulders weren't the only thing on display anymore. His gaze ran down the tapering torso to where Nolan's shorts slid over his hips and muscular ass. He'd had a head start, and in an instant he was naked. And hard.

So damn hard.

Jace finished stripping as Laurel stared. She turned onto her side for a better view of her soon-to-be-lovers. When she saw Nolan's impressive cock and how turned on watching them kiss had made the other guy, she gasped. Her hand wandered down her body, slipping into her bottoms as she said, "Jace. Don't leave him out. Let me see what I missed this morning, or what you two would have gotten up to if I hadn't interrupted."

If that's what she requested, he wasn't about to deny

her. He looked at Nolan, who flashed him a wicked grin as they approached each other. Screw making out—he had better uses for his mouth. One that would serve to get Nolan ready to make this a day Laurel would never forget, one that would mark the beginning of a whole new phase of her life. Jace had no idea if she intended for Nolan to stick around or if this was a one-time show, but just in case, he was going to make the most of it.

Jace dropped to his knees and licked his lips. It put him at eye-level with Nolan's cock, which hung heavy between his thighs. Fuck, he was going to make a mouthful, and hopefully—someday when they weren't concentrating on Laurel—an assful too.

"Fuck yeah," Nolan growled, and put his hand on the back of Jace's head. "You've been torturing me with that mouth of yours, making me watch you sing with Kason every damn day."

Seriously? Jace had been so engrossed in the music he'd been creating with the country star that he evidently hadn't noticed Nolan staring. "I didn't mean to."

Hell, he'd have snuck around back with Nolan for a quick fuck from that very first night he'd met the man. He was edgy and alluring, yet gentle and funny instead of forceful toward those on his side, a combination that Jace found damn near irresistible.

He decided to make up for it right then, his hand reaching out to fist the base of Nolan's shaft, leaving plenty sticking out between his clenched fingers for him to lick and finally suck.

Nolan groaned, his thigh tensing beneath the free hand Jace laid on it to stabilize himself. He took Nolan deeper, letting the blunt head of his cock rub against the back of his throat. He'd long ago learned to suppress his gag reflex, and that skill came in handy when dealing with Nolan's long, thick dick.

"Damn that's hot." Laurel gasped from the bed, drawing Jace's gaze. He flicked his eyes to her long enough to see her removing her own clothes. She tossed her bra at them like a groupie at a concert instead of a woman playing spectator for her two roommates turned lovers. Or one who'd been too shy to get naked first.

If it took showing her his honest passion for Nolan and her to make her comfortable, he had no problems with that.

"Damn, between the two of you..." Nolan trailed off when Jace sucked harder before swirling his tongue over the head of Nolan's cock, tasting the salty musk of precome there. "You're making me glad I work out or I'd have burst a blood vessel by now."

His fingers flexed on Jace's skull, which did nothing to dampen his enthusiasm. He went down on Nolan like the pro he once was, using every trick he'd ever mastered to rev the man up. Not to mention getting Laurel turned on enough to overcome her inhibitions.

After another couple of minutes, Nolan inched toward the bed, dragging Jace with him. His tree-trunk thighs hugged Jace's shoulders. And when he got close enough he said, his voice far huskier than Jace had ever heard it before, "Turn this way, Laurel, if you want me to get you ready too."

Jace mentally cheered, never letting up on his sucking as Laurel flew into place, her ass on the edge of the bed and her torso laying crosswise on the mattress.

Nolan's cock edged into Jace's throat when he leaned forward, taking Laurel's ankles in his hands. He raised them, propping her feet on Jace's shoulders from behind.

From the angle of them, Nolan had tipped her knees out so that her soles rested against each side of his neck. Nolan made room for himself between her legs.

Although Jace's back was to the action as he devoured Nolan and Nolan bent over him to warm Laurel up, there was no doubt about the instant Nolan's lips connected with her flesh. Her toes curled and she moaned, making Jace's cock jerk and a bead of precome slip from the tip.

He redoubled his efforts, swallowing Nolan to the root, the other guy's balls tapping against his chin as encouragement. Not that Nolan seemed to need any. The slick noises that flowed from behind Jace made him sure the agent knew his way around a woman's body and was employing all of his skills to bring Laurel pleasure.

Jace grabbed Nolan's thighs and clung to the bulging muscles there, grateful and excited that this man had finally managed to bridge the abyss of anxiety and bad memories he and Laurel had never managed to cross on their own.

Nolan reached one hand down to rub the back of Jace's head, encouraging him and promising with that touch that Jace was doing as good a job as he thought. He smiled around Nolan's dick and swirled his tongue along the shaft. Nolan groaned and Laurel moaned as the ecstasy Jace gave Nolan transferred to her.

"Damn, you're so sweet," Nolan rasped to Laurel before putting his mouth back to good use.

"You're really good at that." Laurel gasped, then chuckled.

It might have seemed odd, but hearing her laugh while Nolan was going down on her nearly made Jace shoot right then. She was enjoying this. She was into sex with Nolan and with him. Together. There wasn't a single ounce of uncertainty or, worse, fear in her confession.

Holy fucking shit.

Jace couldn't wait until they took her over the top, making her orgasm again and again. He wasn't going to stop giving her pleasure until she asked him to.

"You ready for me to add my finger?" Nolan asked, inspiring Jace's shudder. He was grateful Nolan understood the need to go slowly, cautiously, and that he was so tender with Laurel. If he'd hurt her, Jace wouldn't have hesitated to bite his cock right off and keep him from doing the same to anyone else ever again.

It wasn't an issue.

Laurel couldn't have picked anyone better to break her dry spell with. And Jace thanked the stars that he'd been lucky enough to be included in the moment. Nolan had undoubtedly saved many lives in his career with the Shields, maybe even theirs. But what he was doing right then was something no one had been able to do for Laurel before, and Jace would never forget it.

He held still as Nolan began to fuck his mouth, pumping his cock between Jace's lips even as he feasted on Laurel.

"Oh, yes." Laurel groaned and her feet flexed against Jace's neck as if making sure he was still there. "Your hands are so big."

Nowhere near as big as his dick, babe, Jace thought with a smirk. He got distracted for an instant and choked when Nolan jerked, obviously impacted by Laurel's desire and, most likely, the heat of her sweet pussy hugging his fingers. Lucky bastard.

Jace wasn't going to lie. He'd kept every one of his liaisons to men because there was only one woman he wanted to be intimate with, and she was splayed out across the bed right behind him. He was glad Nolan was there too to make sure she was satisfied, because Jace was going to have a hard time lasting long enough to do the job on his own after what amounted to decades of extended foreplay.

Nolan hummed against Laurel's skin, his mouth making wet slurping noises that did nothing to keep Jace from getting turned on. Apparently Nolan wasn't unaffected either. He put his hand on Jace's shoulders and held him in place before withdrawing his cock from Jace's mouth. The slick thickness of his cock tapped Jace's throat as he gulped down some much-needed air.

Then Nolan said, "Come here, Jace. I want you to see how beautiful Laurel is like this and watch when I make her come on my face."

14

"**F**uck yes." Jace didn't have to be told twice. Nolan went to his knees as Jace climbed onto the bed. Then Nolan grabbed hold of Laurel's legs and draped them over his shoulders. Jace laid face down, perpendicular to Laurel, propping himself on folded arms. He smiled down at her and said, "Hey."

"Mmmm." She blinked her heavy lidded eyes open and stared up at him.

"Is he good at that?" Jace played stupid since there was no way those long swipes of Nolan's broad tongue didn't feel spectacular.

"Uh huh." Laurel blushed and looked away.

No. Jace wasn't going to let her deny what they were sharing. He tipped her face back and when the arousal in her eyes was obvious, he couldn't help himself. He lowered his face and dusted his lips against hers. It was heaven and hell combined, finally kissing her and tasting her parted lips, knowing she wasn't making any sort of commitment beyond this one incredible experiment they were sharing.

It didn't matter if his soul shattered into a million pieces later—he wasn't going to pass up the opportunity to show her how damn much he loved her, and always had, through the most basic and carnal of expressions.

Laurel wasn't simply lying there either. Wasn't afraid or unsure. She was kissing him back, one hand on Nolan's head, pressing it closer to her core—as Nolan had so recently done to Jace—and the other lightly scraping Jace's scalp as she arched toward him and thrust her tongue between his lips.

He sucked on it, reveling in the shudder that rippled through her.

"She's so fucking tight, hugging my hand hard every time you do that," Nolan told him. "She's going to come on me. Soon."

Jace stared down into Laurel's eyes, noting the excitement mixed with awe in them. She honestly hadn't believed this was something she could experience or take joy in, and he was more than happy to prove her wrong as many times as she liked.

"Don't let go," she whispered to him as the peak loomed nearer.

Jace gathered her into his arms, his body connecting more completely with hers, their hearts pounding against each other even as he consumed her sighs and purrs. He took a break only for a moment to whisper, "I've got you, Laurel. *We've* got you. It's okay."

Her eyes flew wide open, and she nodded at him in a few short bobs before her jaw dropped and she froze. Only for a moment. Then her entire body quaked and her abdomen rippled. Laurel rocked involuntarily, shoving her pelvis at Nolan while clinging to Jace.

He peered down at her, so fucking moved that she

would trust them enough to find pleasure with them that he didn't give a shit about his own hard-on drilling into the mattress. At least for a little while. He glanced down her perfect-to-him body at Nolan and hoped the other guy could read the gratitude in his gaze.

Nolan beamed at them both, working his hand in and out of Laurel as he sucked her clit with soft pulls of his lips for the entire duration of her long, rolling climax.

"Damn," Jace whispered to her. "You're even more beautiful than usual like this."

She went limp in his arms and stared blankly up at the ceiling. For a horrifying moment, he was afraid she might cry and her tears would break him. Instead, she cursed reverently, then started laughing even as aftershocks kept her twitching around Nolan and between them both.

"Are you okay?" Jace asked cautiously.

"Why the hell did I wait so long to do that?" She stretched and reached for him, dragging him to her for another kiss. Except this time she wasn't cautious. Her tongue tangoed with his, and she reached for Nolan, drawing him up on her other side before angling her head to kiss him too.

Jace watched for a minute before he had to have a taste of the other man's lips, glossy with the proof of Laurel's pleasure. Their stubbled jaws brushed against each other before they connected fully. And the moment their mouths met, they expressed their mutual relief and pride, ardently mauling each other.

"Damn." Laurel sighed beneath them. "You two are turning me on even more. I think I'm going to need to do that again. And again. And maybe some more after that."

She spread her legs as wide as she could with them hogging her bed, and Jace wasn't about to deny her what she craved. He looked to Nolan, who nodded. "You'd better go first. After that BJ and watching her unravel, I would probably shoot before I got all the way inside her."

That was a possibility for Jace too.

Except he knew how much this meant to Laurel. No matter what she said, this was more than a hookup. It might not be forever, but it wasn't something she took lightly. And neither did he.

As if she could sense the weight of the moment lying heavily on his shoulders, she reached for him and pulled him on top of her lush body. Sure, they shared a bed and snuggled plenty, but this...this was something else entirely. This was touching with intent.

For once he didn't have to try to shift his hips away from her to hide his erection.

Today, he could let her see the desire burning in his eyes.

He hovered over Laurel on straight-locked arms, Nolan caressing the side of her face and then her shoulder, keeping her calm with quiet praise and gentle touches. Despite their caution, Laurel whimpered.

"We can stop right now. Whatever you want." Nolan waved his hands in front of him, and Jace nodded.

Laurel stared at their cocks. Jace's was the hardest he could ever recall, and Nolan seemed like he was in the same predicament.

"That looks painful." Laurel shook her head.

"I'll be glad to take care of him if you want," Jace volunteered.

"Would you hate me if I said I'd rather do it myself?" Laurel looked up at him from beneath her thick lashes. "You know, after..."

"Hell no, as long as I can watch." Jace smiled.

"I'm hoping you'll do more than that." Laurel reached for him. "You were right, Jace. It's your turn. You've always been there for me. I know I can trust you. I know you would rather cut your balls off than hurt me. If I'm going to do this with anyone, it's right that you be first." She glanced at Nolan. "Sorry."

"Nothing to apologize for. Like I said, I need a minute." He came closer and lifted Laurel's shoulders, slipping behind her, hugging her as she reclined on his abs and chest, which became the perfect pillow to keep her propped up and watching what Jace was about to do to her body. "That makes perfect sense. And if you decide that's enough, that's fine too. In the meantime, I'll be here to keep an eye on everything and make sure nothing goes off the rails while Jace is distracted."

"Thanks, man." Jace wished he could have reached Nolan to kiss him again. How had they found someone so big and strong and...fucking kind to take care of them, shelter them, when they needed it most?

"Where the hell did you come from?" Laurel peeked up at Nolan, and the languid kiss they shared did nothing to douse the flames Laurel's confidence and faith had stoked in Jace. "And how do you know exactly what we need to make this work?"

Nolan shrugged. "I'm glad I was in the right place at the right time. Thank you for letting me be part of this with you."

Laurel nodded, then reached for Jace. "Come on. Please get inside me before I lose my nerve."

"You're sure?" Jace asked again.

"Positive." She clutched his shoulder and ground against him, her slick pussy rubbing along the length of his cock. He prided himself on the self-control it had taken to keep his hands off of her all these years, until she was ready, but now that she greenlit them, there was no way he could hold back even an instant longer.

He fit himself to her opening, then groaned as the flexing muscles at her entrance kissed his cock. His hips twitched and he fused them the barest bit together. Laurel gasped and bit her lip hard enough he was afraid she might hurt herself.

"Is this okay?" Jace asked as he held himself above her, afraid to pin her or trigger bad memories. "You can be on top if you want."

"Don't want." Laurel dug her nails into his shoulders, keeping him from retreating. Not that he was about to go any-damn-where but deeper inside her if that's what she desired.

Nolan was there, caressing them both, calming Jace's nerves and keeping Laurel in the moment. "You're doing so good, Laurel," Nolan coached, reassuring her when things might have turned awkward. Jace hated to admit it, but he was glad to have company to make sure he didn't fuck up the best moment of his life.

They both knew he was coarse and unrefined, unlike Nolan who could be suave, though always with a dash of playful, when needed. He'd make sure Jace didn't inadvertently scare her or harm her when he got really into things.

Laurel's breathing evened out. She stared straight into his eyes. "Fuck me, Jace."

He didn't dare tell her that he wasn't going to. Truth was, he'd done all the fucking he cared to do in his life. This was something else entirely. Something scarier and meaningful. He planned to make love to her as he'd always hoped to, not that he'd admit it, because *that* surely would send her screaming away.

He fisted his cock, pumped the shaft from his balls to the tip—where it was embedded in her opening—once or twice to make sure it was good and slick from his own dripping precome and the arousal Nolan had coaxed from her. Nolan hugged her tight, then kissed her forehead as Jace put pressure on the spot where they were connected. He began to slip inside, bit by bit. When she cried out, he froze.

"Don't stop. Don't stop now. Please!" Laurel shouted, then raised her hips, embedding Jace within her. She rocked, impaling herself on him until pure bliss whited out reason and he began helping her fit them together.

Her pussy was nothing like the asses of the guys he usually fucked. Soft, slippery, and so damn flawless he thought he might lose it before he'd hardly worked his way fully into her grip. He looked up and his stare clashed with Nolan's. The other guy grinned, then leaned forward to crush his mouth over Jace's.

He groaned and Laurel clenched around him, clearly not bothered by them making out above her. In fact, she seemed to get off on their show. So he let himself indulge a while longer, his hips grinding against Laurel as his tongue mimicked his movements along Nolan's.

When Laurel whimpered, he peeked down at her.

"She's doing fine," Nolan promised Jace as he carefully studied her features. "Don't worry about that or making her come again. Get yourself off and I'll take over for you."

Laurel moaned and writhed between them as if she didn't hate that idea either.

Jace let himself fly, the last of his restraint eroding in the face of Laurel's passion and Nolan's encouragement. He fucked into her, his hips speeding up gradually until they slapped against hers as he brought them both the maximum amount of rapture he was capable of delivering. He used every skill he'd ever honed to make it good for them both, but before long, he barreled past the point of no return.

"That's right. Come inside her," Nolan egged him on. They were all aware from Kennedy's exams and the tests she'd ordered that they were healthy. Laurel had even gotten on birth control to help with her cramps. There was no reason not to, as long as she didn't object. "Fill her up so I can feel your come on my cock when I slide in after you."

Jesus. Jace looked up at Nolan, their eyes locking just before his balls clenched and he began to orgasm. Then all he could do was chant Laurel's name, and revel in the crush of her arms around him as he unloaded in her. He dropped his head and kissed her, his eyes wide open as he stared into hers, letting her see everything he felt and how much she moved him. Always had.

He gave her the satisfaction of knowing exactly how much she meant to him and how furiously he'd hungered for her all this time.

Jace kept pumping into her long after she'd wrung him dry, until his dick slipped free. Then, groaning, he rolled to his side and curled around her.

"I didn't realize you needed that so badly." Laurel kissed him tenderly on the corner of his eye.

"Needed you," he panted. "Always have."

"I'm sorry."

"I'm not." He angled his face to kiss her again. "You weren't ready. *We* weren't."

"Not until he stepped in and stopped us from keeping

up our bad habits." Laurel looked over at Nolan. "I think
you deserve a reward for helping us out."

"If you're good, I am too." Nolan smiled, though Jace
could see the tension at the edges of it, caused by the
desire raging through him. Jace was usually the one doing
the fucking, but he'd gladly roll over and flash Nolan his
ass if Laurel wasn't interested.

"I'm better than good. I feel like I'm high on you two.
And so turned on..." Laurel was evolving right in front of
Jace's eyes. It was like whatever they'd woken inside her
was stretching and coming alive, never to be shoved back
in the prison it had been locked in for too long.
Thank god.

"I've got you covered." Nolan smacked Jace's ass as if
they were some sort of sexual tag team before tipping
Laurel onto Jace's chest and resituating himself so that he
was in Jace's place.

Laurel's legs wrapped around his hips and she sighed,
instead of cringing, when his weight blanketed her. She
was comfortable with him, relaxed and confident. It fired
Jace up even more to see the effects washing over her.

Nolan rubbed the head of his cock up and down her
slit, slathering himself in her and Jace's mingled slickness
before settling in. His tight ass bunched then released
then tensed again as he worked into Laurel's velvety grasp.

"Damn." He grunted as he thrust, this time burying
himself at least halfway.

"I know, right?" Jace chuckled, thrilled to have
someone who could understand his absolute awe when it
came to Laurel. "Pure heaven."

In fact, his cock was already regretting that it had
ended their turn so soon. It began to stiffen as he watched
Laurel and Nolan come together, both of them lost to the

pleasure they created. Jace dipped his head and sucked Laurel's nipple, his other hand playing with her opposite breast as Nolan really got going.

It salved his ego when Nolan had to clench his jaw and clamp his eyes shut after not too long to keep from losing it inside Laurel. Jace grinned at Laurel, who squeezed his hand. Then Jace leaned in to make out with Nolan. Was he tempting the other guy to fall over the edge? Maybe.

But he also enjoyed swallowing Nolan's moans as he buried himself to the hilt in Laurel.

Laurel raked her fingers down their abs, one hand on each man, and began to chant their names each time Nolan drilled into her. Jace sank down and laid his lips on hers, kissing her tenderly in counterpoint to Nolan's relentless fucking.

And that's when she lost it for the second time, clawing at the sheets and drumming her heels on the bed as Nolan poured himself deep within her. Jace's cock lurched, though he tried to keep himself calm. Laurel might be satisfied. Hell, he probably would have been if Nolan had pounded him so thoroughly with that fat cock of his.

But when her eyes fluttered open, they were still full of steam. She scratched down his chest and said, "More."

Nolan collapsed on her opposite side and began kissing his way from her fingertips up her arm, across her collarbones and finally to her mouth. Jace heard him whisper, "Thank you. That was...incredible."

Laurel hummed, beyond rational thought or conversation. So Jace did as she requested and mounted her. She crossed her ankles in the small of his back, then sucked him into her. He slipped easily inside and took his time, riding her with unrelenting precision and slow, languid glides that extended their ecstasy for longer than he could keep track of.

It was nothing like his hurried booty calls, nothing like the impersonal scratching of a physical urge.

Jace gave Laurel everything he had and hoped she realized that it was a hell of a lot more than only his body he was placing in her care. At some point, she tried to rush him, but he refused until she rolled to the side and took him to his back.

Laurel rose over him like a goddess. She rode him, taking exactly what she wanted while Nolan alternated between feasting on her plump breasts and her parted mouth. Jace planted his feet on the mattress and held on, letting her use him however she needed in that moment. When he started to climb again toward orgasm, Nolan noticed and tweaked his nipple, helping to distract him so that Laurel had what she required to satisfy herself.

Jace groaned and Laurel's motions became jerky.

Nolan rubbed her back and cooed, "That's right. Go ahead, Laurel. Wring him dry. Show him how badly you've wished you could share this with him, even if you didn't know how to tell him."

She cried out then, her eyes flying open as she stared at Jace, her eyes glassy with lust or maybe unshed tears. Maybe both.

And when she caved, her entire body spasming around him, Jace didn't even have to think. His body responded to her rapture, joining her in an epic climax. She milked jet after jet of come from his balls. White-hot heat and the overwhelming weight of reality—they'd actually finally done this—stole every last thought from his mind.

Especially when Laurel melted over him, snuggling on top of his chest while still joined.

She reached for Nolan, who fit perfectly beside Jace, bearing some of her weight. The other man murmured to them both, "That was incredible. Thank you for letting me share it with you."

And right then Jace knew he'd never forget that it was Nolan who had made his most secret dreams come true that day. He owed the man for this and so many other things now that he'd never be able to repay the debt.

Laurel didn't speak, but she kissed each of them, then went limp in their arms, utterly exhausted.

Jace collapsed, his head lolling onto Nolan's shoulder as his heart raced. Not only with physical exertion, but because he realized that by fucking Laurel with Nolan, he'd utterly screwed himself. This wasn't something he could do once and walk away from unscathed after. He'd had enough meaningless sex to know that what they'd shared wasn't only a physical release. At least not for him.

And when he spied Nolan finger combing Laurel's hair before lifting a smug and sappy smile to Jace, he thought Nolan might be having similar thoughts.

Somehow, someway, they had to make this last beyond one superspy mission, because Jace didn't think he'd be able to handle it if their newfound blessings disappeared from his life as quickly as they had shown up.

15

Nolan couldn't believe how time seemed to disappear lately. It had already been three weeks since the day that had changed his life forever, even if Laurel and Jace didn't realize how much of an impact they'd made by opening themselves fully to each other and so generously including him.

Fortunately the house they were sharing—which had previously belonged to Walker, Dane, and Joy from Hot Rides—had a ginormous bed because they'd made good use of it every night since Laurel had blossomed in front of their eyes, and a few times during the day too. Not to mention the shower, the couch, the kitchen counter... pretty much every wall or flat surface in the place.

It wasn't only his temporary home they had become part of, but his whole life. They spent hours each day poring over intel about Draven's operation and tracking down leads. James hung out with Laurel every chance he got, Kennedy and Sola had added her to their group texts and girls' night outing invites, and Kason wrote new, incredible music with Jace every damn day.

They were becoming fully integrated into every aspect of Nolan's world.

And he couldn't say he minded.

He grinned as they rolled up the freshly laid, gleaming black asphalt that wound between the Hot Rods garage and Tom and Ms. Brown's house to the newly finished private complex the classic car mechanics had commissioned. Joe and the rest of the Powertools had really outdone themselves. The place was massive with plenty of room for their ever-expanding family, and was stylish too. It had a modern ambiance to it that kept the trademark aspects of the apartment above the garage they'd been squeezed into before, with concrete floors and exposed steel beams, but the addition of lots and lots of glass and hints of distressed gray wood to soften it from industrial to something Nolan had learned from James was called transitional design.

It made him even more excited to see what James had in store for the new Shields headquarters and attached apartments. The guy had made an exception to his no-more-construction-projects rule for them. Nolan jotted a mental note to beg James to revise some of the specs he'd given the guy for his own living quarters. Add another bathroom and some more closet space...just in case.

He glanced over at Laurel, who was sandwiched between him and Jace on the wide bench seat of the truck the Hot Rods had souped up for him. Then he mentally shook himself as he returned his eyes to the lot as he parked. The place was packed as all their friends gathered for an official housewarming party, now that they'd helped the Hot Rods move in and get settled.

But unlike those people, who'd set down roots, Laurel

and Jace...well, they were only temporary guests in Middletown. He had no reason to assume that their relationship would last beyond the final date of their current mission. They hadn't made any promises to each other. Their affair clearly had an expiration date. Once Draven's operation was shut down permanently, they'd be free to move on without him as their keeper.

Fuck. He needed to remember that before he fell even harder for them. Because one of two things was going to happen. Either they were going to leave, or he was going to have to move on to another assignment, one that didn't involve spending every waking moment with the two people he'd become infatuated with. No more of Laurel's soft snores at night or Jace's heated stares when he was working out. Would they wait for him when that happened? Or would they realize that they were fine on their own and didn't need him anymore?

Nolan wasn't eager to find out.

"You okay?" Laurel hesitated as she took her seatbelt off, picking up on his emotions as usual.

"Yeah, of course. Why wouldn't I be?" He could tell by the way Jace's warm eyes narrowed that he didn't believe Nolan any more than Laurel did.

"I don't know, that's why I asked." She leaned in and cupped the side of his face. "But we're here if you want to talk about it."

For today, sure. For forever, nope.

And Nolan had to be okay with that. He planned to savor every moment they did have together, including today's celebration. "I'll get the gift and the brownies out of the back."

At least he knew how to be helpful and how to make

their lives easier. For now, that would be enough. If he eased this transition to the wonderful new life he knew they were on the cusp of, then he'd at least feel like he had given them something in return for the joy they'd brought him.

Laurel looked at Jace, but he simply nodded and hopped out of the truck before helping her down. If he took a little longer than necessary with his hands on her waist and slid her down his entire muscled front, Nolan didn't blame the guy.

He carried the hand-painted key hanger Laurel had upcycled from an old shoe organizer Ollie and Kate had rummaged for her on one of their recent part-finding and antique-scouting trips.

Speaking of...Kate—who was married to Mike, the head of the Powertools company, and pretty damn pregnant—was right inside the door when they entered. She turned and spied the gift in his hands. Her eyes went wide. Hands splayed on her rounded belly, she made her way to them and exchanged hellos before taking a closer look.

"Oh my God. If I hadn't seen this thing before you transformed it, I wouldn't have believed what it started out as." Kate ran her fingertip over the distressed details. "You have a great eye. I was ready to toss it, and what a mistake that would have been. This will be perfect to organize the million sets of keys they have. They can hang it right here by the door. It looks like it was made for this space."

"Thanks." Laurel seemed a bit reluctant receiving the compliment. "I guess I have a lot of practice turning junk into useful stuff. Giving it another life. Pretty much everything Jace and I have ever owned came off a curb somewhere."

"Well, if this is something you enjoy doing, I've been thinking of hiring help for my business. Especially with our baby on the way—I'm going to need someone I can trust to take care of things when I'm out on maternity leave. Just saying..."

"Are you trying to steal our best server?" Kate's best friend, Morgan, edged into the conversation with Devra right behind. They were grinning, not pissed.

"I mean...I probably pay better." Kate winked.

Laurel flushed. She seemed torn between loyalty and what she obviously enjoyed doing most. Nolan's pulse sped up as he wondered if this was the start of a very tentative, very delicate root. Between this and Jace's work with Kason, maybe they wouldn't be in such a hurry to skip out of Middletown after Draven had been eliminated.

"I hope you know we're teasing." Devra slung an arm around Laurel's shoulders and she didn't even flinch. She was comfortable here. With him and with the extended circle he'd been fortunate to join as well. "If you want to spend your days dumpster diving with Kate, have at it."

Laurel snorted. "Since you make it sound so appealing, I'll think about it."

She peeked up at Jace, who was beaming. The other guy squeezed her hand and she smiled back. Every time Nolan witnessed the link between them and their unspoken conversations, he had to wonder when they were going to realize they didn't need a bodyguard to keep them safe from each other and kick him out.

So it surprised him when Laurel reached for him too. Fuck it, he wasn't going to discourage her when he wanted nothing more than for them to have a reason to stay, even if it wasn't him right at first...or ever. "I think it sounds smart. You're really good at this."

"Thank you," Laurel flashed him a wide, genuine smile. The sort he hadn't seen from her very often until lately. She was morphing right in front of his eyes, exactly like the key holder. Reborn. Refreshed. Ready for a new phase of her life.

Nolan set the gift on the metal table, big enough for an army, which Wren had welded and given to their Hot Rods cousins as a final touch on the new home.

Laurel was distracted from their heavy discussion by the appearance of her brother.

"Hey, big sis."

She rushed to James and crushed him in a hug as if she would never get used to having him in her life again. It got Nolan every time. And Jace too. The other guy shuffled until he stood shoulder to shoulder with Nolan. Jace leaned in and murmured, "You literally have no idea how amazing that is. We owe you guys everything."

Nolan wished he could have kissed Jace then and told him exactly how much more he'd like to give the other guy and his soulmate too, since he hadn't even scratched the surface, but it didn't seem like the right time or place for those sorts of confessions. Later, he promised himself.

Behind James, a woman with straight black hair and an impressive array of facial piercings carried a baby swaddled in a flame-covered blanket. Eli, the Hot Rods garage owner, and his husband, Alanso, hovered over her shoulders. "Congratulations, you three! First the baby and now a new place with plenty of room to spread out."

"We're lucky bastards and we know it." Alanso's Cuban accent grew thicker as he studied Sally, Eli, and their baby boy, Maceo. "Want a tour? Maybe it'll give you some ideas for your own apartment. I heard James is coming out of retirement to hook up the Shields."

"I am. I am." James clapped his hands, then rubbed them together. "I know I said I didn't want to be a foreman, but I'm not trusting anyone else with a place I have to work in every damn day. It doesn't make sense for us to be trekking up to Kason, Jordan, and Wren's place in the ass end of the forest every time we have a meeting. I could be spending that time at home, with my family."

"Getting laid, you mean." Eli chuckled and so did Nolan.

Laurel scrunched her eyes closed. "Not my baby brother."

"Hey, I'm not the only one getting plenty, by the looks of it." James whipped his stare between Laurel and the two obviously satisfied men flanking her. It still twisted something inside Nolan that everyone seemed cool with it. Like maybe if it worked for them, that was all that mattered. Huh.

Nolan couldn't help himself. He fell back on his bad, jokester tendencies to get a single jab in. "I promised you I'd take care of your sister. Isn't that what you had in mind?"

"And....*there's* the line." James shot him the finger before addressing the larger group. "Okay, truce. But yeah, I am working on the new building going up in Middletown. Shields business on the ground floor and plenty of apartments for our expanding team and any witnesses or temporary peeps we need to find shelter for, who require plenty of protection, all in one place. I even talked Jordan into an indoor pool and hot tub adjoining the gym facilities. It's going to be epic. I've never worked on a multi-story commercial building like this before.

Especially not one that will become the tallest in Middletown. Not going to lie, it's kind of fun, but only this once."

"If you don't mind talking shop later, I'd like to make a few tweaks to the plan we'd discussed before everything is finalized," Nolan blurted before he second guessed why he suddenly wanted to turn his apartment from a bachelor pad into something a little more trio-friendly.

"Of course you do." James rolled his eyes, but the effect was less harsh when he grinned. Was Nolan that obvious? "That's fine. There's someone I wanted to introduce to you guys anyway. Well, Nolan already met him under less than ideal circumstances, but Laurel and Jace..."

Nolan already knew who James was referring to. The kid had been glued to James's hip since they'd rescued him from the hellhole not substantially different from the ones Laurel and Jace had grown up in. Eli, Alanso, and Sally wandered off, swallowed by the milling friends surrounding them, promising to show them around when they were ready.

James weaved through the crowd until he found a teenager with an unruly mop of brown hair and brought the kid back with him. Nolan imagined James probably hadn't looked so different at that age. "Mark, this is my sister, Laurel, her friend, Jace, and you remember that big guy, Nolan, I'm sure. Meet my apprentice, Mark."

"I've heard a lot about you." Laurel held her arms open, shocking both Nolan and Jace, whose open jaw gave Nolan lots of ideas for later. "Can I give you a hug?"

"Sure, I guess." Mark's words might have been hesitant, but he cuddled up to her and squeezed before he'd finished speaking. Given his upbringing and the fact that he was now living at Tom's youth shelter when he wasn't spending time with James, Nolan figured the kid would soak up affection like the crunchy toffee biscuits Laurel liked to dunk in her coffee, the ones he'd paid Devra to keep a constant supply of in the bakery case.

Nolan could attest that Laurel's hugs were basically magic.

She ruffled his hair, then let him go slowly. "I heard you were part of the reason James got tipped off about where Jace and I ended up. Thank you. So much. I owe you everything."

"Me?" Mark blinked up at her, clearly enamored.

Totally understand, kid, Nolan thought.

"Yeah. You were brave as hell," James told him, squeezing his shoulder. "And the things you remembered helped us track down the people who hurt Laurel."

"I didn't do hardly anything." Mark shrugged one bony shoulder. "But I'm glad some of the shit I've seen made a difference." James cleared his throat and Mark grimaced. "Stuff. I meant stuff."

Jace smothered a laugh at that. "You must have a lot of potential if James is showing you the ropes. Construction work is a decent job. You're going to be okay now. On the right path to a better life with so many years left ahead of you to make something of it."

"Thanks." Mark shook his cascade of hair back as if he didn't feel the need to hide behind it anymore. He smiled sheepishly up at James, who was obviously his hero. "I'm hoping that after we're done with the Shields project I'll be ready to join one of the other Powertools crews."

"Part time." James nodded. "You have to finish school before you can come on permanently, but if that's what you still want after graduation, I know a foreman and a forewoman who owe me some favors..."

Nolan, Laurel, and Jace snickered at that.

A roar broke out from somewhere in the back where the giant family room took up a large chunk of the main floor along with the entry, dining room, and kitchen. Hoots and hollers, along with a few whistles, drew them —curious—in that direction.

16

―――――――

"What's going on back here?" Nolan heard a familiar buzz. He rubbed his forearms and the ink covering them as he remembered what it felt like to have the artwork permanently etched into his skin. Not so different from how he felt every day longer he spent with Jace and Laurel, who were indelibly imprinted on his heart and soul.

Wren filled them in. "Mike is building a tattoo shop downtown for our friend Blakely, but until it's ready she's been doing house visits with her mobile set up so we thought we'd hire her for the party. The Hot Rods are each getting matching tattoos tonight. Nothing elaborate. The garage logo, about the size of a quarter. Eli teased his dad about doing it too and Tom called his bluff. He's sitting for his first ever tattoo tonight."

Nolan grinned and Laurel clapped along with the rest of the gathered gangs. Tom was a father to most of them, not only Eli. It meant a lot for him to do this for his son. For all of them. It proved what he told them so often, that he was proud of what they'd built together both professionally, and more importantly, personally.

Tom whipped his black long-sleeved T-shirt over his head and everyone cheered again. Especially his wife, Ms. Brown, who fanned her face dramatically. Damn, that was no dad bod Tom was sporting either, even if the fur on his chest and flat stomach was silver instead of dark like his son's.

He straddled the bench across from Blakely. Her own father, Giovanni, who had commissioned the tattoo parlor and tourist hub not too far from where James was breaking ground on the Shields headquarters, put his hand on the up-and-coming artist's shoulder and squeezed.

Nolan wondered if his parents would have been even a fraction as supportive and proud of him if they'd survived long enough to see him become a hired assassin. He hoped they would have understood his purpose, but he was constantly weighing the terrible things he had to do against the good they resulted in to make sure he wasn't becoming like the people he took out.

Laurel put her hand in his. "It must be nice to know someone loves you that unconditionally, huh?"

Jace shot her a look out of the corner of his eye. Did she seriously still not understand that she already had that, with Jace? Or was she referring to the unwavering support of a parental figure?

Either way, she must have tripped Jace's instincts. He edged closer to the tattoo station, peering at the first bold swipes of Blakely's gun over Tom's chest. He didn't so much as flinch, staring out at the roomful of people he'd inspired and damn near raised on his own.

From beside them, Nolan heard Mark whisper, "Badass."

"Can anyone get a tat tonight?" Jace asked no one in particular.

Blakely glanced over at him when she paused to dip her gun in the miniature plastic inkpot. "Sure. I'm here the whole night." She returned her attention to her work on Tom and asked, "Are you another virgin, like Tom?"

"Honey, it's been a hell of a long time since Tommy was a virgin." Only Ms. Brown could get away with calling him that. Her heated stare and the way she licked her lips as she studied his fresh markings made it clear she appreciated his experience and benefited from it regularly.

"*LA LA LA*. Not listening." One of Ms. Brown's grown daughters, Amber, stuck her fingers in her ears and rotated toward her husband, Gavyn, who owned the Hot Rides motorcycle shop—the sister garage to Hot Rods—burying her face in his chest to block out the steamy signals her mom was sending Eli's dad.

Nolan boomed out a laugh. He'd never been part of a group where everyone was so accepting and open-minded, or—for that matter—so damn happy. Life goals.

His boss, Jordan, stood nearby with his husband, Kason, and their wife, Wren. When Nolan looked up, he caught Jordan's raised brow. Yeah, it was probably pretty obvious Nolan had never been this content either. Shit.

"Jace has quite a few tats already," Laurel answered Blakely as she raked her gaze down the sinew of his forearms.

"None as high quality as yours." Jace practically drooled as he studied the rock-solid line work of the design Blakely drew on Tom. "Mine were mostly exchanges for bouncer work or because I signed up to be the guinea pig for artists starting their training. Never could afford that kind of talent."

"We can now," Laurel murmured to him. "I know you've been wanting to get a new piece."

"They are addictive." Jace cupped the back of his neck. "And there is something I've been thinking of a lot lately."

"How big? How involved? Party tats are usually quick and small, one or two colors max." The woman looked up again, her head tipped a bit. If her long ash-blonde hair hadn't been wound into some sort of messy bun it would have cascaded over her shoulder. She was as beautiful and tough as the art she created.

Jace pointed to a three-inch gap on the front of his arm. "Nothing major. Looking at these, you could do it in your sleep."

"Well, then take a number and get in line." She beamed up at him, transforming her down-to-business look into an inviting one that Nolan might have locked onto if he wasn't already fully entranced by Jace and Laurel.

"Thanks." Jace grinned, a rare full-on smile that punched Nolan in the gut. Damn, they were going to be here celebrating for hours, but he couldn't wait for their private after-hours party later.

"Um, could I too?" Laurel shocked them both by asking. Nolan had seen every inch of her creamy skin and could attest that she was a blank canvas.

"Of course," Blakely said without hesitation.

"Really?" Jace turned to her. "You've always said there wasn't anything you were so sure about that you'd commit to it for life."

"Things change, Jace," she said, then sighed, a calm coming over her that Nolan hadn't seen before.

"They do." Jace kissed her forehead and smiled as he rested his cheek on the top of her head. Nolan stood behind. Though he probably shouldn't have, he couldn't help himself from wrapping his arm around them both for a group hug.

James glanced over at them and flashed Nolan a thumbs-up from outside of Laurel's peripheral vision.

It didn't take much more than twenty minutes for Blakely to finish with Tom. When she wiped his chest clean, before wrapping the area, he stood and showed the group his Hot Rods tattoo. The room erupted again, and Eli slapped his dad on the back in a one-armed hug, careful not to smoosh the new tattoo. He cradled Maceo in the crook of his free arm and Nolan could see how a family like this could be so strong, generations of badasses looking out for each other and teaching them how to survive.

Eli knuckled the corner of his eye. Kaige, one of his Hot Rods buddies and sometimes lover, ripped on him for getting soft in his old age. But it was only shit talk, nothing serious. The whole gang gathered around and admired the artwork, which matched their own.

Blakely smiled and gave a self-satisfied nod, then turned to Jace and Laurel. "So what did you two have in mind?"

At the same time Jace said, "I want her name on me," Laurel said, "I want Jace's name."

They turned and stared at each other before breaking out into laughter.

Nolan chuckled with them until he realized it was probably too soon for him to ask for both of their orders.

He cringed. He'd be willing to ink their names on his half-sleeve or his soul permanently, right then. But he didn't think either of them was ready to hear that. So he stared enviously at their matching grins and imagined a time when he might have the right to ask for that sort of forever commitment.

He held each of their hands as they subjected themselves to Blakely's needles. Laurel got Jace's name surrounded by music notes on the inside of her wrist, and Jace wore Laurel's name along with a vine of thorny blood-red roses. Nolan didn't let his envy ruin the moment. He snapped pictures for them and thought it was perfect. They belonged together.

He only hoped that he might be able to share in their bond for a little while longer.

When Blakely finished with them, Jace bent down and smothered Laurel in a sexy kiss. Nolan captured that moment too. If nothing else, he'd have the photographs to look back on when they were gone or he was spending a night on the ground, waiting to ambush some unlucky asshole.

Before he could get too gloomy, Sabra and Holden's twins sprinted between them, using him as a shield in whatever game of tag they were playing. Foam darts launched from a toy gun flew in their direction and he caught them without thinking, making Jace's brow arch at his reflexes, which kept them unscathed even from children's toys.

It would be good to remember who and what he was.

Although they enjoyed their friend time, the conversations, and the food—damn, the food he was going to have to work off the next day—as the hours wore on, he grew less and less patient, eager to have Laurel and Jace to himself.

"Hey, Nolan." Ollie approached as he put his coat on, clearly as ready to seclude himself with Van and Kyra as Nolan was to bail with Laurel and Jace. "I have those crickets you asked me to pick up when I got Mr. Prickles' food from the pet shop earlier."

"Oh, awesome, thanks." Nolan smiled, the perfect excuse. He asked Ollie, "You want us to come with and pick them up? I'm sure Dottie Long-Tongue will enjoy them. She seems to hate her fruit-only diet."

Laurel beamed up at him. "You got my lizard bugs?"

"Yeah. I know what it's like when you're used to the good stuff. Can't get enough of it and nothing else will ever measure up."

"Did you imply my sister is like a juicy cockroach?" James tipped his head with a snicker. "You're going to have to do better than that if you ever want to move into tattoo territory."

Nolan smacked his forehead. "That's not what I meant..."

But it sort of had been.

Ugh. He was fucking this up.

"I think it's really nice you thought of her. Thank you." Laurel didn't hesitate—she went onto her tiptoes and kissed him softly. Or at least it started that way, but one taste led to another...

Jace cleared his throat. "I think we better go make that pickup and get home."

Nolan separated himself from Laurel, unable to speak.

"Thanks for coming. It's good to see you three doing so well." Eli saw them to the door. "Our house is always open to friends. You're welcome anytime, and I hope you'll take us up on that often."

Nolan nodded, clasped Eli in a brief guy-hug, then looked at Jace and Laurel.

"That goes for all three of you." Eli grinned. "You're family now, and the sooner you accept it, the less awkward it will be."

Laurel beamed and Jace shook hands with the garage owner. "Thanks, man."

Nolan could tell from the gleam in Eli's eyes that he wasn't joking, though. Nolan wished his implications were more than a hunch and that he could end up as fortunate as his friends living this twisted-fairytale life.

For the first time in a long time, Nolan thought it might be possible that his dreams could come true, with a bit of luck.

Laurel ducked under Nolan's arm and held her other hand out to Jace, who laced their fingers together as the three of them made their way to Nolan's truck and...he was pretty sure...straight to bed when they arrived home.

Screw the bugs.

17

Jace leaned toward Nolan so that their shoulders rested against each other as Laurel splayed out across their laps on the not-quite-big-enough couch watching some dumb movie that couldn't hold his attention when he had them to stare at instead. He didn't mind one bit. Nolan's warm muscles flexed against his every time he laughed, and he wondered if tonight might be the night they finally gave in and fucked each other instead of lavishing their combined attention on Laurel.

Not that he'd minded nearly a month of worshiping her and building her confidence, acclimating her to the physical aspects of their affection. But he'd be lying if he said he hadn't been eyeing Nolan's tight ass in his skintight shorts when he'd returned from a bike ride that had provided his daily dose of cardio earlier. Sure, they kissed. Had jerked and sucked each other off plenty, but for some reason neither of them had made a move to sink into the other.

Maybe it was because keeping Laurel satisfied once

she'd unleashed years of pent-up passion took every drop of their energy, but for whatever reason they'd set some kind of boundary and it didn't seem like they were going to be able to move forward until they smashed through it.

He surveyed Nolan from the corner of his eye and sighed. It had taken him damn near twenty years to figure shit out with Laurel. He didn't want to make the same mistake with Nolan. Not when things had been going so smoothly that he'd nearly forgotten this was only temporary.

Fuck.

Jace clenched his jaw.

Nolan turned toward him and frowned. He put his hand on Jace's stubbled cheek and brushed his thumb over his lips. "What're you thinking about?"

Jace drew a deep breath as Laurel blinked up at him, catching on to the atmosphere between the two men. It was time for him to come clean, to admit that he hoped they could keep things going for more than however long it took to finish their job here.

But he should have made that decision sooner.

Because just then someone pounded on the door.

Before he'd registered the repeated thumping, Nolan had already slipped from the couch and tucked Laurel into Jace's arms, then crouched and whipped his phone from his pocket to check the surveillance camera aimed at the porch.

He grunted, then flung the door open. "Shit, James, what's your problem? You almost got your ass kicked."

James brushed Nolan aside, his smaller stature no hindrance when his energy was so overwhelming. He snuck inside and turned to face the three of them. "We've had a breakthrough. It's go time."

Jace had known Nolan was a warrior from the first instant he spied the man stalking Laurel at Heels. He drove it home when he straightened, every muscle and instinct on high alert, like a predator very comfortable at the top of the food chain. Nolan was a trained killer, as lethal as he was easygoing day-to-day and generous in bed.

"You came in person to tell me that? Why?" Nolan's shoulders locked into place, his stance widened and every glorious muscle in his body went rigid.

James flicked his gaze between Laurel, Jace, and Nolan, then took a deep breath before saying in a rush, "You remember the woman you and Sola talked to during the cannery raid? Turns out she is pretty incredible. She had a chance to go free, but instead decided to come on as a mole. She's been the one feeding us info from the front lines."

"Wait, do I know her?" Laurel stood, so Jace did too, all of them forming a ring around the coffee table in the small space.

"I think so. She told me where to find you." Nolan winced.

"Her name is Cherri," James told Laurel with a sigh. "And she needs our help. She arranged for Draven to be alone, separated from most of his goons for a brief window, tomorrow."

"Cherri!" Laurel clasped her hands, then brought them to her chest. Jace's guts twisted. She'd been their friend. Volunteered the knowledge that had led Nolan to them. And she'd refused the chance to get the fuck out? What the hell?

"How exactly did she manage that?" Nolan was

obviously a few steps ahead of Laurel and Jace on this one.

"She might have promised him something." James cleared his throat and looked away at Dottie sunning herself in her cage-castle on the kitchen counter.

Oh no. Jace knew whatever it was, he was going to hate it.

"She swore to Draven she knew who has been picking off his higher-ups one by one these past months. She didn't have a choice—he was going to kill her. So she told him about the Shields and that we're working with Laurel and Jace."

"Son of a bitch!" Nolan punched his own palm hard enough that Jace thought he wouldn't be able to play guitar for a week if he'd done the same. Laurel angled herself toward him and put her trembling fingers on his bunched biceps.

"It's okay. Sometimes you have to do what it takes to survive in those situations." Laurel looked up at him with a shallow smile. "We're fine. We're protected here with you."

"You won't be for long." Nolan growled. "You're right, James. We've got to put a stop to this once and for all. Now. So who's going in? Who did she offer to arrange a meeting with in order to isolate Draven? Jordan?"

"Uh...nope." James stared at Nolan.

"Me? Fine. I'll do it. But why would he give a fuck? He doesn't know who I am, and let's be honest, around Shields I'm only another soldier on the team."

"Not you either." James waited for realization to dawn.

Jace snarled. "So help you, if you say Laurel right now, I'm going to lose my shit."

"No!" Nolan bellowed. "Absolutely not."

"What?" Laurel blinked.

"It's a fucking trap." Jace flung his hands out, karate chopping the air.

"Of course it is." James rolled his eyes at Jace. "But we only need an opening. A single chance and Aarav will take the shot. This will be over, for good."

"You want to use me as bait?" Laurel asked James, her voice low though without a quiver.

"I don't like the idea of you doing it. But I also don't own you and I'd never act like I did. So I'm bringing this possibility to you and letting you decide." James held out his hand, and Laurel clasped it in hers.

"Thank you. For really understanding me." Laurel smiled sadly. "Of course I'll do it. The risk is worth even the chance to end this nightmare. Not only for us but for every life he's infected with his evil. And you'll be there, right?"

She turned her gaze to Nolan, her beautiful eyes wide and trusting despite everything they'd gone through. How? How could she have faith in anyone anymore?

Every last shred of Jace's faith burned to ashes and floated away on the blast of cynicism that followed. "You two swore to me that if we stayed, we wouldn't be in danger. That Laurel wouldn't be involved. You fucking lied to us. To me! The pile of money you gave us 'for information' means nothing if we can't trust your word. Hell, Nolan. We even slept with you, for Christ's sake!" Jace whipped toward Laurel next, glaring. "Don't look at him like that."

"Like we're in a shitty situation that we need to find a way out of together? Like I care for him?" Laurel reached across Nolan, but Jace evaded her gentle touch. He didn't want to calm down. Didn't intend to listen to reason. "I do. And so do you."

"No." Jace waved his hands in front of him. "Not if he's willing to put you in danger after he swore he wouldn't."

James cleared his throat. "It isn't how we normally operate, but we have an obligation to Cherri. Plus our own agents. Draven is closing in. Hunting us as hard as we're chasing him. If we don't make a move on our terms, we could very well find ourselves being picked off next. The absolute worst case scenario is for him to come to Middletown looking for you."

"Why? Because then *your* loved ones would be at risk?" Jace sneered.

"Laurel is my blood. And I consider you part of our family," James encapsulated the three of them with his stare. "And I know Nolan does too."

Nolan cursed. "I don't like this plan any more than you, Jace, but James is right. The rest of the team will be in on the op too. If it was someone else, anyone but you two, I'd be making the same argument James—and the rest of the Shields, because he didn't come here on his own—is."

That didn't alleviate any of Jace's turmoil, especially because he didn't like the idea of Nolan being exposed either. At the end of the day, this was what he did. Who Nolan was. And if he fell in love with the guy, he'd have to accept that.

Fell in love? He barely restrained himself from cackling maniacally. No matter how this turned out, they were fucked. Their feelings were already involved, even if they'd been pretending otherwise. *Shit.*

"There's something else you should know. I'm not suggesting you should instantly be okay with this if you're not because of what I'm about to say, but you should have all the facts before you make a decision..." James took a step back from Jace as if he was afraid of earning himself a black eye.

Jace canted his head.

"If you thought being an informant paid well, you're going to pass out when you see the raise you're being offered. Agents make about a hundred times your previous salary considering the risks involved. There's also a substantial death benefit, not that we hope to ever pay that out. If you do this, you won't have to worry about starting over afterward. Anything you want, you'll be able to make it happen. That degree program you mentioned, Laurel, you wouldn't even notice the tuition missing from your bank account."

"Serving Draven a huge helping of justice pie would be payment enough." Laurel waved James off. "If it saves even one kid like me, like Jace, like Mark, like Cherri, from having their childhood destroyed, then I'm in. For free."

"Nah, that's not how it works around here." Nolan took a deep breath, then blew it out slowly. He looked at the awe and admiration in Laurel's eyes and nodded. "If you choose to do this, I'll have your back."

Laurel seemed to melt, triggering Jace to lash out. He wasn't about to let her be blinded by lust only to doubt her own judgment later. He couldn't stand to see her crushed when her loyalty was violated again.

"Would you please quit looking at him as if he's some kind of saint or our savior?" Jace spun to face Laurel and Nolan directly, blocking out James shaking his head in Jace's peripheral vision. So what if Laurel's brother was in Nolan's camp and not Jace's? Could he lose her to the other man after everything they'd been through?

Hell no, wasn't happening.

"We've been living in some fucked up fantasy, Laurel. He's no hero! How do you think they stop these guys? By asking nicely?" Jace flung up his hands. "Laurel, you're falling for a fucking murderer. You get that, right?"

James winced. "Trust me, they prefer if you don't use the M word."

"Fine. He promised to protect you and now he's putting your life on the line. If fucking around with you in this bullshit bubble these past months ruins the best thing in my life, I will regret this for the rest of my days." Jace snarled, making Nolan stagger back. "No piece of ass, however fine, is worth losing Laurel. I knew this was a stupid idea! Fuck!"

Laurel stared, her gaze shifting between him and Nolan. "Jace, how can you say that?"

"He's not wrong." Nolan hung his head, his broad shoulders slumping. Somehow that only made Jace feel worse.

"Yes, he is. Look, Nolan might kill people *who deserve it* for a living, but at least he is willing to show affection and...well, whatever else, to those he's close to instead of letting them wonder if they're good enough for him." Laurel took a stance next to Nolan.

"You think I don't love you? Is that what this is about?" Jace grabbed his hair as if he was about to yank it out.

"No." She stared at him like he was an idiot, and maybe he was, but she might as well have been speaking another language for all he understood what she was really getting at. "I know you do. But..."

Jace stepped closer. "Isn't that enough?"

"I don't know. You never say it, and we haven't exactly made any promises about what's happening here. What if you get bored or decide you want to go back to hooking up with other people? What if you only want me as part of a package deal with Nolan, but once the novelty wears off, he bails?"

"What?" both Nolan and Jace croaked simultaneously.

"I've had the best months of my life here with you two and I don't regret a single thing. But if I don't do this, I'll never be able to live with myself or believe I deserve anything that comes after." She turned to James then. "Tell Jordan I'm doing this."

"It looks like you three have some shit to work through first." James pointed to the bedroom. "Jordan is coming in from the mountain house to meet with everyone in the Hot Rods dining room, since they're at work and it doesn't make sense for us to keep trekking up to the Hawk's Nest constantly. That means you have two hours before you need to report in for duty. I suggest you use them wisely."

Jace swallowed hard. His hands shook. Partially out of frustration, yes, but also out of terror. Everything was slipping through his fingers. And he wasn't the sort of man to stand back and let go. No, he needed to fight.

James leaned in toward Laurel and hugged her tight. "Everything's going to be okay. Listen to your heart and don't be afraid to chase your wildest dreams, okay? No matter what, you've got me, Laurel-loo."

She patted James's back and nodded. "I love you, little bro."

James looked at Nolan. "Two hours. Don't be late."

Jace stalked to the bedroom, angry and annoyed though secretly glad when Nolan and Laurel's footsteps followed close behind.

18

Laurel's head spun. Just like it had the day they'd first come to Middletown, everything had changed in an instant, except this time definitely not for the better.

It wasn't fair. She'd started to feel at home and forget what it was like to worry every day about how they were going to survive.

She trotted after Nolan and Jace as they stalked to the bedroom and shut the door quietly behind them. No one was leaving until they'd hashed out whatever had come to a head out there. She was not about to lose the progress they'd made over this. Draven was not going to steal one damn thing more from her.

In some ways, though, Jace was right. Nolan had promised they'd be sheltered, far from the action. And no matter what sort of ninja operative he was, he couldn't be certain they'd emerge unscathed if he took them with him to the front lines. That didn't mean she was going to bail. Not on Cherri and not on the chance to stop Draven from wrecking another person the way he'd nearly broken her and Jace.

No way.

She bit her lip as she imagined Nolan with a gun in his hand, taking someone's life, his usual disarming grin nowhere to be found. He did bad things, *very* bad things, even if it was for good reasons.

Laurel took a second to weigh it out. On the other hand, she'd known plenty of high-profile, powerful men, who were praised for their donations to charity or contributions to society but were actually a cancer to humanity. Nolan was the opposite of that. So was she okay with it?

Yeah, she was.

Nolan rambled, seeming off balance for once. "Look, I'm sorry it's come to this. I didn't anticipate it would and totally understand if you're not interested in putting yourself in this position. Sola could be made up to look like Laurel from a distance, and one of our guys can stand in for Jace since Draven won't expect her to come without him by her side."

Laurel snorted. "No one is going to mistake that siren for me."

"Sometimes I wonder if we live on the same fucking planet." Jace turned to her, exasperation making the corner of his eyes wrinkle. "And you..." He stabbed his finger into Nolan's chest. "Might as well quit wasting what time we have. She's made up her mind. It's done. We're in this now."

"Fuck." Nolan kicked the bed hard enough to make it thump into the wall. "I don't like it either, Jace. You have to know that. I can't stand the idea of either one of you anywhere near that sick bastard."

"And you?" Laurel asked, still quietly refusing to let the storm brewing between the guys suck her in.

"This is my job." Nolan looked over his shoulder, cringing. "You've known that since we met. Is it a problem all of a sudden?"

Why did he look like he'd been expecting this, or something like it?

Laurel crossed to him and wrapped her arms around him. She refused to let any of them walk into peril with their personal life crumbling around them. "What's really going on here?"

"My job is hazardous. I accept that. I figured that if something went sideways for me you'd still have each other. You'd be fine without me." Nolan shrugged as if it was a casual comment despite his voice shredding. "But I couldn't live with myself if something happened to you or to Jace. I couldn't handle it or face the other knowing I hadn't done my job to protect you both."

"Well, then let's make sure the three of us come home in one piece. And we can figure out the rest when we do. Okay?" Laurel didn't wait for their assent—she started ditching her clothes. It might not have been a sexy striptease, but it was efficient.

Nolan and Jace quit eying each other with mistrust and rage and despair. Instead, they focused on her as they had so many times during the past month. Laurel realized then that she'd been selfish. It was time to show them they could be more.

"I'm sorry, Nolan," she whispered as she trailed her fingers down his jawline.

"For what?" He scratched where she'd touched. "Don't you dare try to let me down gently. If you're over me, say so. I always knew you and Jace would realize you didn't need me."

Why were men so dumb sometimes? Laurel barely refrained from rolling her eyes like James so often did. Meanwhile, Jace was shooting Nolan an incredulous stare that she could get behind.

"I fucked up. It turns out, I haven't been entirely honest with you either." Laurel sighed. "See, I'm not really capable of casual affairs. I never could be after what happened in the past."

"I understand." Nolan swallowed hard. "I figured this was coming eventually. And I swear I will hunt Draven to hell itself if I have to in order to make sure he pays for what he's done to you."

There was his "bad" side. And damn if she didn't find it kind of sexy in an edgy sort of way.

Jace still gawked at Nolan as if he was dense. "No. You don't. She's telling you she has feelings for you. We both do. So make sure your fine ass doesn't have any extra holes in it at the end of this thing."

"Oh." Nolan's eyes dilated, his energy shifting as he went from retreating to offense. "For the record, this is the only thing I've ever had that lasted beyond a one-night stand or a weekend fuck-a-thon."

"Someday, when we have a lot more than two hours, I want to talk to you about why that is." Laurel cupped her breasts. Then she ran her hands down her sides to help shimmy out of her leggings. No longer was she the least bit shy about being nude in front of Jace and Nolan, no matter what they were wearing.

Besides, it didn't take long for them to get the hint. They practically ripped off their clothes before capturing her between them, Jace at her back and Nolan plastering himself to every inch of her front. Their warmth chased away the chill that had invaded her when she'd realized that she was going to have to risk her future to be done with her past once and for all.

Hell, she'd been willing to charge into the midst of things alone the night Nolan had found her. Found them. Going in with the three of them together, and the rest of Jordan's team as backup...well, the odds were much better than they ever had been before even if they still weren't great.

She refused to think about that. Not until they left this room and faced reality together. Until then, she intended to show both Jace and Nolan how damn much she loved them.

Oh shit.

Laurel drew Nolan to her for a kiss to keep herself from blurting out her revelation. The last thing they needed was for her to complicate the situation even further before they had to concentrate in order to stay alive.

If the silky glide of her lips over Nolan's was tinged with desperation, she was sure he would understand. If they weren't careful, this could be the last time they ever tasted each other.

Jace's arms wrapped around her, holding her close to his heat and hardness as if he would never let go, no matter how Draven tried to rip them apart. Something shifted inside Laurel. No longer afraid, but angry. No longer timid, but assertive.

She nipped Nolan's lower lip, encouraging his groan before shoving him toward the bed.

He tipped onto it, then reached for her, but she didn't go to him, not yet. Instead, she ordered Jace to join him. "Lay there, side by side."

His brows rose, but he did as she commanded. Laurel climbed onto the mattress, standing so that she towered over the two men spread out before her like a sexy buffet. She ran her hands over her own body, thrilled by the way their eyes tracked her every motion. Their cocks were hard and thick as they rested across their tight abdomens.

And she couldn't resist touching them even one more second.

She sank carefully to her knees, straddling both of their touching thighs. Laurel stared at them as she rocked, rubbing her wet, aching pussy on their corded muscles. Then she reached for them, her left hand stroking Nolan's shaft while her right hand pumped Jace.

The men shared a heated glance with each other before they moaned.

Laurel chuckled then leaned in. "Jace, take over for me."

He didn't hesitate, brushing her hand aside so he could jerk Nolan off while she turned her full attention to his erection. She couldn't remember ever seeing it quite so stiff, the veins standing out in relief, or as deeply rouged. As she admired him, a bead of precome dotted his tip. She licked it off, slowly, letting the flat of her tongue caress the head of his cock.

He cursed and his fingers clenched on Nolan's shaft. Nolan thrust his hips and fucked through Jace's fist. Oh this was going to be fun.

Laurel smiled before taking Jace into her mouth and surrounding him with soft heat. Over the past month, she'd learned so much about each of these men, what they liked, how to prolong their lovemaking and how to push them past their admittedly impressive self-restraint. She put every tidbit of that knowledge to good use as she serviced Jace. As she sucked him, she peeked up at Nolan, who was staring at where her mouth intersected Jace's body while Jace stroked his cock.

It only took a few bobs, where she sank low enough to lip Jace's balls while his cock stretched her jaw, before he tapped out. "Too much more of that and we're not going to make it to the main event."

Laurel pulled off him slowly, with extra pressure, before turning to Nolan, who was laughing.

"Think you can do better?" She arched a brow at him, reveling in the power it gave her to hold their pleasure in the palm of her hand, or her mouth.

His head fell back before Jace reached over and tipped it toward him. And when the two guys began to make out, Laurel made her move. She didn't jump right to going down on him, instead laying a sneak attack on his balls, nuzzling and licking them until his sac drew tight to his body before finally sliding down his shaft, swirling her tongue along it as she went.

Nolan uttered a strangled sound that Jace happily swallowed. To even the score, Laurel took Nolan's hand and guided it to Jace's cock. It didn't take more than a nudge to give Nolan the right idea, and soon his hand was working Jace's erection in time to her own motions over Nolan's cock.

Watching them kiss, observing how eager and not very careful they were with each other, turned Laurel on. She rocked faster against their legs as she treated Nolan to a killer blowjob.

Her orgasm caught her by surprise, going from a dull

rising arousal to full on fireworks when Nolan tore his lips from Jace's and begged for mercy. "Stop. You gotta stop or I'm going to lose it. You're so fucking good at that. And Jace...God!"

Knowing that she could do this to them, amp them up and turn them on, prime them until they were as wild for her as she was for them...it did things to her.

Laurel rose up, her back arched, and she came so hard she would have toppled if the guys didn't reach out, Nolan grasping her shoulder while Jace put a hand on her waist. Their touches only protracted her pleasure as she quaked in their hold, her core rubbing over their joined legs to wring the most rapture possible from her climax.

"Sorry." She breathed heavily. "It caught me off guard.'

"Never apologize for enjoying us." Nolan stroked her hair.

Jace hummed in agreement. "I'll never get tired of seeing you like that. In fact, I'd like to watch you come again, as soon as possible."

He leaned forward as if he might turn the tables and press her to her back on the bed to feast on her. Laurel was too far gone for that. She needed more than his mouth to satisfy the need growing within her, urged on by the fact that this could be the last time they were lucky enough to be together, all three of them, whole and in...lust.

"Enough." Nolan growled. "Let me up. I need to fuck."

"Me too." Jace raised his head enough to catch a glimpse of the slickness Laurel had left there, glistening on his bunched thigh, before letting it drop to the pillow once more with a groan.

As much as Laurel loved teasing them and driving

them wild, she was happy to hand them the reins because truth be told, she needed her men inside her as badly as they longed to be there.

19

Nolan tried desperately to be suave, to remember all the things he'd learned about how to please a woman and a man in bed. He wished he was patient and generous, but instead the only thing he could do was obey the demands of his body and his heart. If he was about to lose Jace and Laurel, either to Draven—god forbid—or to their time together coming to an end, he had to make the most of this last liaison.

He tried to burn every moment, every touch, every twinge of excitement into his mind so he could replay this encounter over and over in the long, lonely nights ahead.

Jace moved even faster than he did. He bowled Laurel over and took her to her back on the bed. She shrieked, the laughter that followed ensuring she enjoyed his unrestrained display rather than being frightened by it. Both of them had come such a long way in the past month. Nolan wasn't sure if he had a right to be, but he was incredibly proud of them.

For a moment, Nolan knelt beside them, admiring how gorgeous each of them were, Jace's blue-black tattoos

—gritty and unpolished, genuine—hugged his lean build, standing out in stark contrast to Laurel's creamy skin. He stared as Jace wrapped his fist around his cock then aimed it at Laurel's steamy core.

They went for it.

Nolan's dick twitched as he imagined what it would feel like to be Jace working into Laurel's hot pussy, bare. It didn't take much effort since he'd done it last night and many others before that, but he'd never get tired of that sensation and the sparks that first contact set off in his entire being.

Laurel gasped and arched her back, wrapping her legs around Jace to draw him closer and sink him deeper within her. She clawed at his shoulders, and Jace didn't hesitate to give her what she so obviously craved. His ass flexed as he powered into her then withdrew. The tight globes did nothing to make Nolan any less hard.

He stroked himself as he watched Jace ride Laurel with long, sure strokes that he wouldn't mind being the recipient of sometime either. *Fuck.* He hoped he hadn't wasted his chance, but they'd been so focused on Laurel and bringing her out of her sexual shell that he and Jace hadn't gone all the way with each other.

If this was it, the last time he got to spend with the two people he had come to adore, he wanted it to be as epic as his feelings for them. Jacking himself off until he sprayed them with his release while they unraveled in each other's arms wasn't what he had in mind. But neither could he hold out any longer.

They'd spent entire nights loving Laurel together, but in that moment, Nolan lost every scrap of his finesse and patience. Self-control went out the window.

"I can't wait. I need to fuck." Nolan inched toward the

head of the bed, and Laurel licked her lips as if offering her mouth to him while Jace occupied her pussy.

At the last second, Jace stopped him. "No. Wait."

Nolan froze and looked at Jace, who was still tunneling within Laurel's heavenly body.

"Fuck me instead."

His heart stuttered and his cock lurched. Now? Did he want to, hell yes, but for some reason—by some unspoken agreement—they hadn't crossed that line before, giving everything they had to make up lost time and pleasure for Laurel.

Nolan looked to her then, afraid to discover jealousy or hurt or even disgust.

He shouldn't have worried. She writhed beneath Jace and screamed, "Yes!"

"You want me to fuck your lover?" Nolan had to be sure. He caressed her face, dipping his thumb into her mouth for her to suck and nip. The last thing they needed right then was more confusion or anything that might drive a wedge between them. They had to stand together, and with unwavering strength.

Although, being honest and exploring could bring them even closer. And while he didn't like the idea of gambling when it came to their security, his instincts were screaming so loud, he couldn't ignore them. They had to do this. He would lay down his life for theirs if necessary, without hesitation.

But if it came to that, at least he'd have experienced this one special pleasure first.

Nolan lunged for the nightstand and drew out the tube of lube they'd used when they'd pinned Laurel between them, both of them filling her. Sometimes both in her pussy or sometimes one in her ass while the other glided deep into her, stroking the other through the thin wall of tissue separating them.

Tonight was going to be a whole other level of intense. Their emotions were running on high and so were their desires.

Nolan slicked his cock before applying a liberal amount of the gel to his fingers and sidling up behind Jace. The other man widened his stance, pressing Laurel's thighs farther apart with his knees as he made room for Nolan behind them in bed.

Nolan ran his hand down Jace's back from the nape of his neck to the swell of his ass, capping off his caress with a slap. He'd been dying to do that for a while now. Jace grunted and ground deeper into Laurel before withdrawing, tipping his flank up as if asking for more.

So Nolan gave it to him, spanking him a few times in rapid succession before soothing the rosy area with a gentle massage. He used his grip to spread Jace apart, then guided his slicked fingers upward from the base of his balls to the tempting hole that clenched in response to the cool air rushing over it.

Nolan circled the opening, making Jace curse and twitch, his motions growing jerky as he fed Laurel his cock. And when Nolan pressed his middle finger inside, he thought Jace might sear him. Jace shuddered and looked over his shoulder before begging, "Hurry, Nolan. This feels so good already. I want you inside me, joining us, before I lose it."

"I don't want to hurt you."

"I can handle you. Come on." Jace pressed back, his ass swallowing Nolan's finger. He added another and then a third, gently spreading them until he was sure Jace could take his cock without pain.

Laurel helped out by running her hands over Jace's shoulders and kneading his chest, distracting him with sweet kisses and breathy encouragement. It must have worked because when Nolan set the slippery head of his cock at Jace's entrance, the other guy jumped.

"You sure you're ready?" Nolan wondered. No matter how loudly his dick objected, he'd stop right then if there was even a hint of uncertainty from Jace.

He shouldn't have worried. Jace looked over his shoulder, his expression fierce. "Yeah. Get that dick in me already. Fuck me, Nolan. Fuck us."

Laurel moaned, only encouraging Nolan's forward motion. And then he was there, pressing into Jace bit by bit until the other man's ass sheathed his entire erection. His balls tapped against Jace's, his pelvis shoving Jace's ass so that he, in turn, drilled deeper into Laurel.

The three of them cried out at the same time, each of them enhancing one another's ecstasy.

Nolan had never done drugs, but he figured he could understand how someone could get addicted to the rush if it felt anything like the sensations pounding through his veins with every beat of his heart. At first he moved in counterpoint to Jace, fucking into him as the other man retreated from Laurel. But after a few minutes, their motions became hastier and less coordinated.

Then he pinned Jace to Laurel and picked up speed, letting more of his weight rest on his lovers. As he bottomed out in Jace, Jace pressed into Laurel.

Nolan loved his position on top of them so that he could watch them going at it as he plunged into Jace. It would only have been sweeter if he'd been tucked between them instead of watching from the outside.

One step—or fuck—at a time, he promised himself.

Nolan clamped his hands around Jace's trim waist, anchoring himself so he could drive deeper and harder through the tight ring of muscle hugging him. When Jace groaned and shuddered, he knew he'd hit the right spot.

Laurel beamed up at him. "He loves that, Nolan. Do it again. He's so hard inside me, and when you fuck into him, he does it to me. Damn."

Her eyelids fluttered as she tried to keep them open while pleasure bombarded her. She and Jace made out, their hands flying over each other and sometimes what they could reach of him. It didn't take too long before Laurel's eyes widened and her stare locked on his.

"I'm close."

"Me too." Jace groaned as if he'd been hanging onto the edge for a while already.

Nolan was right there with them. He pumped into Jace, slapping the side of his flank as he really got going. Laurel gasped and Jace clenched around Nolan, dooming them all. They flew past the point of no return.

This time they came together. Nolan flooded Jace's ass, triggering the other man's climax. He overflowed Laurel's pussy with his release, pumping into her until she shouted and tossed her head from side to side. While Nolan couldn't feel her contractions wringing him dry, she inspired aftershocks in Jace that made his ass clench on Nolan, transferring her rapture to him.

He came so hard, he was pretty sure he'd almost turned his balls inside out.

The only thing that could have been better would have been to be the center of their universe, the man in the middle.

Still, he wasn't greedy, and he was thrilled they'd shared this much of their lives and their obvious love for each other with him. Laurel kissed Jace and reached up to put her hand on Nolan's shoulder, petting him as he remembered how to breathe.

He'd be forever grateful that he'd found them, and that by doing so, they'd found him.

Now he had to keep them alive long enough that he could tell them so when it wouldn't be a massive distraction and risk getting them killed.

20

Jace chewed his index fingernail until the iron tang of blood washed over his tongue. What the hell were they doing?

"They're two minutes out." James's voice rang through the earpieces the entire team wore. "Remember, everyone: Laurel and Jace are a diversion. We only need them to get us an opening and then we'll take that bastard out however possible."

"He picked this place on purpose, that's for sure," Aarav grumbled over the comms. "It's surrounded by trees. I have a very limited window to pick him off, and I'm guessing he's aware of that."

"I'm sure he is." Laurel sighed. It seemed like she was resigned to things going to hell, same as Jace. It was the only way he could see this ending.

Someone was going to get hurt. Or worse. He only hoped it was Draven and not one of the people Jace had come to think of as family. He peeked into the side mirror through the dark-tinted window of the SUV Laurel was driving. There was no longer anyone right behind them.

Sola and Nolan had peeled off a while back, circling around on a parallel road and getting into place in the woods with Kennedy and Marcus, Ransom and Levi, and a couple pairs of fresh recruits he'd barely glanced at during the briefings. He'd been too busy staring at Laurel and Nolan, terrified that it would be the last time he had the luxury.

Every instinct he possessed screamed this was a horrible idea, but it was the only way they'd put an end to their nightmares for good and truly be free. Besides, Cherri was there, still in Draven's clutches. They had to try to get her out too. She deserved a shot at a life beyond hell, one as amazing as his and Laurel's and Nolan's had been these past several weeks.

"We're in place." Nolan's mission-voice bore no resemblance to the friendly, lighthearted timbre Jace knew so well. Soldier Nolan was a stranger to him. Cold, focused, and lethal. Right now, that made him feel the tiniest bit better.

"All set here too," Marcus confirmed.

"Same, boss. Ready to roll." That kid sounded like he was barely old enough to see an R-rated movie, never mind be hunting criminal masterminds. He sure did seem excited about it though.

Jordan came on. "Remember, Teddy, you're mostly eyes and ears. Don't engage. Stay back and watch out for any incomings behind the teams on the ground unless I specifically tell you and your partner otherwise."

"Yes, sir." He sounded like he might have been pouting, though he didn't argue.

"For the record, I still hate this." Jace couldn't help but get one last word in, though there was no way Laurel would change course now. Honestly, she was right and—as usual—braver than him to recognize it.

"Me too," Nolan grumbled.

"Take it easy," James coached. "Get out there and keep him talking until we can figure out an angle. Before you know it, you'll be back in bed with Nolan and my sister and you'll never have to worry about this again."

It was the part in between exiting the car and being at home in his lovers' arms that was freaking Jace out, but he nodded to no one anyway.

Laurel reached over and covered his hand. He squeezed her fingers, then brought it to his lips before murmuring, "I love you."

"I love you too," she answered before either of them thought about their vows being broadcast to the rest of the team, Nolan included.

Jace cleared his throat, unsure if he should shout out to the other guy while he was on the clock and laser focused. And then the moment passed. They spotted the turnoff to the clearing ahead, and suddenly the anticipation phase was over. It was go time.

"They're pulling in now," James told the rest of the Shields. "Everyone on high alert. Let's get this done as quickly as possible. Be safe, Laurel-loo."

"Will do," she answered before putting the SUV in park.

Jace circled around the vehicle and helped her down even though she didn't need his assistance. He'd rather wrap himself around her and keep her from being so much as seen, never mind exposed to the man responsible for the agony they'd endured.

The one who was standing not a hundred feet away in

the center of a small clearing, definitely *not* in line with the tiny gap in the trees that would have cleared Aarav to take a head shot and finish this before it began. *Fuck.*

"Haven't seen you two in a while. You're looking good," Draven called with a smirk as they drew near, but not *too* close to where he stood with Cherrie by his side. He scanned Laurel from head to toe. In addition to being a pervert, he was smart. "Come here."

Every instinct Jace had rebelled. He didn't want that immoral fuck touching Laurel. Nor did he like the thought of Laurel anywhere near the trajectory of Aarav's shots. The Shields respected the fuck out of the sniper, but the margin of error there was too damn small.

Laurel hesitated, but Draven grabbed her wrist and yanked. She crashed into his chest. Jace could smell the overpriced cologne the man practically bathed in from his position a few feet away. He didn't blame Laurel for gagging when it smacked her in the face.

"Fuck," Aarav snarled through the headpiece. "I've got him in my sights, but he's not an idiot. If Laurel so much as flinches, I could tag her too."

"Hold," Jordan commanded.

Terror paralyzed Jace. A tiny flicker of motion over Draven's shoulder caught his attention. He tried not to look, feeling more than seeing Nolan stalking through the shadows. He had to believe the man was going to keep them safe as he'd promised he would. He'd never let them down yet, but this felt wrong on every level.

"Enough chitchat," Draven snarled, any hint of civility vanishing in an instant. "Tell me who's after me. Here I was kind enough to let you two go, and you repay me by siccing rabid dogs on my business partners? You were ancient history. Why now?"

Laurel shrugged. "We're living our own life. Maybe you should mind yours."

Draven slapped her across the face, making her head whip to the side.

Jace growled and stepped closer.

"Don't! He's got a gun!" Cherri screamed at them, sealing her own fate. The last words she got out were, "He's not alone either!"

And then Draven shook his hand down, his gun falling out of the sleeve into his hand. With one motion, he took her out. Cherri didn't even have time to make a sound before a dark spot blossomed on her forehead.

NO!

In the tree line, a commotion broke out. Fighting amongst the soldiers on either side of this invisible war. Jace wondered how often shit like this happened and people were oblivious, going about their day-to-day lives without any knowledge of the seedy underbelly of the world swirling in the shadows around them. He wished he could be that oblivious. That he wasn't watching Cherri's lifeless body drop to the leaf-covered ground in slow motion. Suffering over in an instant.

Aarav hissed a curse, then a tree exploded in the distance and Jace was sure the sniper was covering Sola's ass with his large caliber rifle rounds. It wasn't like he could help Laurel, not with her entangled with Draven. Close enough to make Jace's skin crawl. The gun in his hand, now aimed at Laurel, meant there wasn't a damn thing he could do. Instead, he stood there, helpless.

Chaos erupted around them, leaving them to weather the eye of the storm with the one person he hated most on the planet. Something inside him snapped.

"I'm going to draw his attention to me. Get Laurel out

of here," he breathed, hoping the comms could pick up his warning.

"No!" Nolan bellowed. Jace heard him in stereo—both through his earpiece and from not as far away as he would have thought in the clearing.

Jace didn't listen. It was too late. He was already in motion. The instant Draven glanced toward the noise Nolan had made, Jace charged.

Draven whipped his hand up, gun pointed directly at Laurel's heart. But a roar that could have belonged to a Viking warrior or some prehistoric animal in agonizing pain ripped from Nolan. He exploded through the underbrush, diving in between Draven and Laurel.

He jerked when a bullet smashed into his chest and a second hit him a bit higher as he crashed to the ground. All Jace could see was the wash of blood that ran like a curtain down Nolan's neck. But before Draven could pull the trigger again, Jace tackled the asshole while Laurel screamed Nolan's name.

It happened even faster than the gunshots. Jace barreled into Draven, taking him down. The gun clattered from the other man's hand. Nolan didn't even reach for it. Instead, he somehow levered himself up, then planted his knee on Draven's sternum. He wrapped his hands around Draven's neck and wrenched, putting every fiber of muscle he'd built up during his endless workouts to use.

The sick sound that echoed through the clearing was one no amount of music would ever erase from Jace's memory. If there was any doubt as to what Nolan had done, the fact that Draven now stared wide-eyed in a completely unnatural direction, almost directly behind him, would have clinched it.

Instead of dying down, more motion surrounded

them. Shields poured from the trees and overtook each of the hired guns, who stared in shock, the head of their organization decapitated. Almost literally.

"Jordan! Teddy's down." Sola's flat tone said plenty.

James confirmed anyway, "Does he need medical assistance?"

"Too late." Sola cursed.

Jace's stomach heaved as he realized the cost of their operation.

Cherri... Teddy...

Nolan?

The stakes were high for the Shields. No matter how skilled and experienced they were, they weren't all coming home. Not this time, and likely many others. There was a reason governments, organizations, and who knew who else gave Jordan enough money to set them up for life.

None of the bounty they'd come into would matter if they lost Nolan now.

Jace scrambled toward him. Laurel had already rushed to Nolan's side. He lay gasping on the ground beside Draven's lifeless body, clutching his chest. It was hard to see what damage there was through the spray of blood squirting from his neck.

"Nolan!" Laurel wailed, clasping her hands over his wound as if she had any chance of stemming the rush of blood.

Jace blinked, the sight of crimson dripping between her fingers planting the seeds of nightmares he would live with for years to come. He knelt beside his lovers and stared into Nolan's pretty eyes. He leaned in and fixed the other guy's always-perfect hair.

The corner of Nolan's mouth tipped up despite his ragged breathing and groans.

Then Kennedy was there, shoving Jace aside. Marcus was one step behind her, approaching Laurel, gently shooing her away. "You want me to keep the pressure on?"

"Yes. Take over for Laurel. Your hands are bigger. When you swap, I'm going to wipe him off and see what we're dealing with. Then I'll know what we need to do next." Kennedy was brisk and efficient, already hauling things—bandages, a clamp, and other shit Jace didn't know the purpose of—from her medical kit. He hoped that she stayed in hyper mode. As long as she was resourceful, flying through her routines, he had a sliver of hope.

Jace couldn't be standing there watching the man he loved bleed out. Not now. Not when they'd barely found each other and especially not when Nolan had saved their lives. Again.

He'd done it once before when he'd brought Laurel and Jace together. When he'd gently popped the bubble of denial they'd blown around themselves.

As Sola stepped up and tried to guide them back a few feet, giving Kennedy and Marcus room to work, numbness overtook Jace. Laurel collapsed against him, burying her face in his chest as she sobbed, unable to watch Nolan suffering, dying, right there before them. Jace clutched her to him.

Nolan's blood smeared across Jace's arms and shirt when Laurel broke down, grasping him as if he would be able to keep her steady when Nolan wasn't there to do it for them.

He wasn't sure that was possible. Not anymore.

The truth was, if Nolan didn't survive, neither would their relationship. They would never overcome the guilt and grief he would leave as his legacy. Even their love for each other wouldn't be able to fill the holes in their hearts.

21

Nolan groaned. His arm was stiff. Probably trapped under Laurel or Jace, the pitfall of sharing a bed with two lovers.

Wait. *Laurel! Jace! Draven...shit!*

He would have bolted upright except the discomfort in his arm radiated down to his chest and up to his neck. He realized it wasn't due to a cramped muscle but the direct hit he'd taken to his body armor, which had undoubtedly saved his life even if he'd still cracked a rib or two. Motherfucker. He pried his eyes open and checked for holes in his wickedly bruised torso, finding none. When his fingers grazed the section of his neck that felt like it was on fire, they were met with bandages most likely covering stitches and burns.

Draven's second shot had grazed him there, sending a streak of lightning across his flesh that had made him pretty sure he was a goner.

Holy fuck. That had been a close one.

"Awake?" Jace asked quietly from behind him in the dim light of dusk or dawn, he had no idea which.

"Yeah." He didn't even try to roll over. That would have been too much effort, which meant he was probably under the influence of a painkiller or some sort of sedative. Who knew what Kennedy would have pumped into him to keep him comfortable.

Nolan hummed when Jace's fingers ran through his hair, stroking it as he'd seen the other man do to Laurel's when she roused from fitful slumber on the verge of a nightmare. He didn't even give a shit that it probably looked like trash instead of his usual patented flip.

"Do you need anything? I've got some water here. More pills. A granola bar..."

"Gotta piss." Nolan winced. The last thing he wanted was to get up, especially if it meant leaving Jace behind, but there was no helping it.

"You've been out for most of the day. Hang on. I'll help you up." Jace rolled from bed and to his feet with the agility of a jungle cat, making Nolan feel like an overgrown oaf when he couldn't coordinate his limbs properly. He paused only to drop a light kiss on Laurel's forehead where she dozed on the pillow beside his.

"She's going to be pissed. Her eyes only closed a few minutes ago. She's been staring at you the whole time as if she doesn't believe you're still here." Jace winced, then ducked, looping Nolan's arm around his shoulders.

"I can make it on my own," Nolan grumbled. "Not the first time I've been hurt on the job, you know?"

"Probably better if I don't think about it." Jace sighed and practically carried Nolan to the bathroom in their bungalow at Hot Rides.

When he'd finished and washed his hands, he seemed steadier on his feet, though he didn't move Jace's arm from its half-hug, mostly because the comforting weight reminded him they were still here. Still together. At least for the moment.

Jace ushered him back to bed and fluffed his pillow. They were careful not to jostle each other both to keep from irritating his sore muscles and so that Laurel could catch up on her sleep. Face to face in the soft light, Nolan studied Jace's eyes, surprised when the other guy hardly met his stare.

"I'm sorry for the shit I said when we found out about the meet-up." Jace looked like he'd been burning with regret since the moment he'd rightfully reminded Laurel that Nolan was a murderer.

"Why? You weren't wrong. I slaughtered that fucker and I didn't even feel bad about it. Still don't." Nolan would have shrugged if his shoulder weren't buzzing with masked pain.

"Yeah, well, if I'd had the chance I'd have killed him too." Jace leaned in and brushed his lips over Nolan's. "I'll owe you for the rest of my days for saving Laurel. I couldn't live without her, you know that."

Nolan wished he didn't remember the gun pointed at her or the flash from the muzzle that had blinded him as he'd leapt, unsure about whether or not he'd been soon enough. "I didn't do it for you. I did it for me. But I'm glad it went the right way. It was entirely too close. Fuck."

"It worked out. I should have trusted you. I'm sorry." Jace winced. "I'll try to be better about that from now on."

Nolan touched a faint scar on Jace's cheek, brushing his thumb over it. "I know how Laurel got mixed up with Draven's trafficking, but...what about you? What happened? Who let you down?"

"My parents, I guess. Dad bailed before I was in kindergarten, not that anyone made me go to school much anyway. My mom shopped around for a replacement with a chain of guys, anyone she thought had enough money to get us by. When I was ten, she found someone who wanted her, but not her baggage. She moved in with him and I wasn't invited. Came home one day to the apartment empty of her shit and the landlady asking for rent."

"Son of a bitch!" Nolan growled, wishing he could rewind time.

Jace shrugged. "It wasn't so bad. I fended for myself on the street, living in parks in the summer and surfing couches when the weather got cold. I wasn't a teenager for long before I realized I could earn enough to feed myself and get a room somewhere on the coldest nights by charging for BJs I would have given for free in the park bathrooms anyway. Or for letting some of the creepy older guys jerk me off. It was easy money."

"No. No, it wasn't." Nolan opened his arms and let Jace decide if contact would be helpful or harmful right then.

Their hearts beat against each other when he snuggled up to Nolan gingerly and sighed. "It was better than when I got a little older and started getting beat up and stiffed instead of paid. Or when guys a lot bigger than me wanted more than oral and decided just to take it. So when one of Draven's guys decked a jerk, got me my cash, and promised to cover my ass for a cut... Well, I was stupid and took him up on it. And when he convinced me to go to a party where I could work somewhere clean and fancy as fuck instead of next to a toilet that hadn't been cleaned in three months, I signed up for that too. I just didn't realize it was a one-way ticket."

Nolan rocked them as Jace painted a picture that made him wish he could kill Draven all over again.

"I like to tell myself it was worth it because I found Laurel. Whether either of us likes to admit it, she needed me same as I needed her. I wouldn't have survived those years without her." Jace closed his eyes briefly.

Nolan smoothed the lines in his brows until he blinked his eyes open again.

It surprised him when the mattress dipped behind him and Laurel rotated to fit herself to him, stretching. Their talking must have roused her. She kissed his shoulder softly, whispering his name. The spirals she rubbed along his spine with her fingertips eased his discomfort.

"I was ready to give up before you appeared and made us a team." Laurel reached across Nolan and cupped Jace's cheek.

"But you didn't. You're a fighter." Jace turned his face to kiss her palm. "And so is Nolan. I love that about both of you, even when I don't deserve you. I'll do my best not to let my scars fuck me up so badly that I can't fully put my faith in both of you now. I do, it's just...in that moment, when things started to unfold...panic overtook logic. I'm sorry."

"I understand." Nolan leaned in and kissed Jace. "You've only ever been betrayed before, except by Laurel. You expected the worst from me, but I swear to you that if you'll let me, I'll spend the rest of my life proving that I'm not like every other man who's ever been a part of yours."

Nolan took a deep breath, then put his heart on the line. It beat faster than when he'd leapt in front of Draven's bullet. "I don't want to be just another hookup you can keep at arm's length because you're afraid of being betrayed or disappointed. If you let me, I'd like to love you—both of you—and hope that I never let you down."

He rotated his head as far as his sore muscles would allow so that he could peer up at Laurel too. A tear spilled from the corner of her eye, sailed down her cheek, and splashed onto his shoulder.

Nolan rolled to his back so he could clasp one of each of their hands as they bracketed him in bed. "I mean, unless I've done my part by bringing you two together. If that's what my purpose was, I understand and I'm grateful I could do it."

"You're trying to get out of this?" Jace raised a brow, nearly falling back into old habits. "Nah. You're not. You're scared. You dumbass, don't you understand?"

Laurel swatted Jace's shoulder over Nolan. "Don't call him names. He's hurt. And this is partially my fault. You two spent so much of your energy making me comfortable..."

"I've enjoyed every minute of the past weeks." Nolan stopped her from going down that road. "If you got something out of it, then I'm happy, even if it means that you're ready to go out on your own with Jace now."

"That's what I'm trying to tell you. There is no us without you. There never was and there wouldn't be now." Jace looked toward Laurel, who nodded. "Being around you, feeling comfortable, having someone to bridge the gaps between us and push us when we both get stuck... That's what finally made this possible. It only works because of you."

Jace cleared his throat when his voice turned ultra-raspy. "So don't be leaving us now. Not because you're nervous and definitely not because you let some piece of shit like Draven put a hole in something vital."

"Does me being part of the Shields freak you out?" Nolan felt exhaustion creeping over him like a heavy blanket. They had so many hurdles in their path.

"Upset? No. More like impresses the hell out of me." Jace frowned. "Although I'm torn up for Teddy's family, and will probably lose my shit every time you're away from us, I wish I was half as capable as your team. If I had been, maybe I wouldn't have ended up where I did."

Suddenly Jace's fierce independence and his scrapper nature made so much more sense. Good thing Nolan never had been deterred by those rough edges.

"On a personal level, I love spending time with them, especially Sola and Kennedy." Laurel grinned. "I could learn a thing or two from women as strong as them. And the guys too. Including James, of course."

"You do? Yeah, you do." Nolan's head hurt as he tried to consider the possibilities, but he couldn't deny that Jace and Laurel had already melded into his network of friends.

"Don't overthink this." Laurel rubbed his back.

"Okay." He turned off the destructive voice reciting the reasons it couldn't work. "In that case, do you guys want to move in with me when my place is ready? You could hang out with James and...the rest of the team. And...you know, me. All the time. When I'm gone, you'll have other people around, which will help me overcome my guilt for leaving. Plus, they'll look after you, too. I mean, not that you need it, but I would be less anxious knowing you were covered."

Jace laughed, damaging Nolan's heart a bit. Was it so ridiculous?

"Did you think you could get rid of us?" Jace leaned in

and kissed Nolan while Laurel kept caressing his tensed shoulders.

"I don't like to make assumptions..." Nolan held his breath as he looked to Laurel.

"It's not like we have anywhere else to go." She shrugged. "I already told Kate I would accept her job offer, and the Powertools will be using this place as a showroom for their tiny home offerings starting next month."

"But that's not the only reason, right?" Nolan hated the doubt he couldn't fully erase. He wanted Laurel and Jace in his life, permanently. But he couldn't be on the outside looking in forever or he'd never survive.

"Of course not." Laurel grinned as she shoved him lightly. "I'm teasing about that last part. Didn't you know, being an agent for the Shields is a good gig if you can get it? I'm pretty sure I don't need to work for the next five years, if I don't feel like it. And I might actually take some time off once Kate is back from maternity leave if I end up going to school. Ms. Rodriguez, the director at Tom's shelter, said she'd be happy to write a reference letter for me if I want to apply to the social work program at the community college here. With the experience I'm getting during my volunteering there, and her backing, she thinks I have a good shot at getting accepted. No matter what, we're not going far. And I could hire James's husband and wife to build me a whole village of tiny homes without putting a dent in our bank account."

"Good point." Jace smirked. "And that's even before we count the advance Kason is giving me since he signed me as a permanent member of his studio band."

"He did?" Nolan hugged them. "That's great news. Both of you. You deserve it. Laurel, you can change the world. Jace, you make Kason sound even better."

"Thanks." He smiled, and for the first time since Nolan had met him, it felt like it reached all the way to his soul. The man was content, some of the anxious edge fading away. Though he was still plenty sexy in his bad-boy rocker sort of way. "I believe this is where we were meant to end up, what we're meant to be doing. But none of it matters without you. As awesome as a custom tiny home from the Powertools would be, none of those places would come with a smoking, bisexual assassin with a big dick and perfect hair like you."

Nolan laughed at that, or started to until his body told him it wasn't the greatest of ideas. Despite the stiffness in his torso, he was glad Jace and Laurel hugged him to keep him next to them in bed when he felt like he could float away at any moment. Could this really be true? Could he have what he'd been too afraid to dream of?

"There was one other thing that happened while you were out of it that you should probably know about." Laurel rolled up the sleeve of her pajama shirt, which he realized was one of his button-downs. It swallowed her, but it touched him that she'd wanted to be wrapped in his scent when he'd been out of it.

Jace didn't bother with subtlety. Instead he whipped his long-sleeve T-shirt over his head, making Nolan very aware that they were cuddled up in their bed and that the aftereffects of the buckets of adrenaline his body had produced during the raid hadn't quite worn off.

Jace and Laurel lined their arms up so he could see the tattoos they'd gotten of each other's names. And there, above each of theirs, was his own. A heart with a dagger through it replaced the o in Nolan, making him sure they fully accepted both his profession along with their relationship being something real and lasting.

"Holy shit." He licked his finger and scrubbed it across the bright blue fading to navy on Jace's skin, but it didn't come off. It was the real deal. He was part of them and they had claimed him, right there for everyone to see.

Laurel cracked up. "It's not temporary, Nolan. Blakely made a quick house call for us."

Whether she was talking about the artwork or their relationship, he figured it was true for both.

He reached for them, dragging them to his chest and crushing them with his shaking arms, aches and pains be damned. "I love you too. Both of you."

Nolan would have said more, but Jace's mouth was there, kissing him with less urgency and more finesse than usual, as if he knew they had eternity and didn't have to rush anymore. His gaze was steady when it met Nolan's before he broke the kiss so Laurel could have a turn. She was sweet and gentle, though no less determined than Jace.

Nolan had never been surer of anything. He'd found his home. Here, between them.

"When I thought we'd lost you..." Laurel's whisper cracked, shredding Nolan's heart along with it.

"Shh. You didn't. Not this time. I can't promise you won't ever though. Are you sure you want to sign up for that?" Nolan knew this could be the part of him they couldn't accept. And he wouldn't blame them. Was he willing to give it all up to stay with them?

Yeah, he would if that's what it took to have his soulmates.

Jace took Nolan's chin in his hand and angled his face so he couldn't ignore the truth blazing in the other man's eyes. "We love you for who you are. For your heart and your sense of what's right."

"For fighting for those who can't do it for themselves," Laurel added, touching her hand to his chest over his heart. "We would never ask you to change for us."

"Oh. Okay then." Nolan was sure he should have come up with something better than that to say when they eased every doubt he'd ever had about finding not only one but two incredible people to share his bed and his life with. He knew in that moment that they were a set, never to be broken apart.

"So to celebrate, I think you should let us love you," Laurel murmured, already flicking the buttons on her top open one by one.

"I'm not going to argue." Nolan sighed. "Except...I hope you don't mind if I'm kind of lazy about it."

Jace snorted. "I'm surprised you can get hard at all."

"That's not a problem." Nolan looked at his two lovers then down at his steely cock. With them touching him, telling him everything he'd ever wished for was within reach, it had refused to lie dormant.

"Then lie there and let *us* take care of *you* for once." Laurel kissed him languidly as Jace carefully removed Nolan's sweats.

Finally, there was only skin on skin on skin.

Slow movements and lots of long, sensual kisses. Caresses and sighs.

No sense of urgency. They had an entire lifetime to love each other. Again and again.

Nolan had no idea how many hours they spent like that, locked together, simply soaking up the positive energy and endless pleasure they could bring each other. But eventually he needed more.

From where he rested on his side, Laurel in front of him and Jace spooning him, he shifted and his cock tipped upward. Instead of sliding between Laurel's thighs, where she'd been cradling him, he pressed the barest bit inside.

"Mmm. Yes." Laurel adjusted the angle of her hips to fit him more completely within her.

Distracted by her tight heat, Nolan didn't realize Jace had retrieved the lube from somewhere and slathered his fingers with it until they began to search around his ass.

Nolan groaned.

"Is this okay?" Jace asked.

"Dying for you to fuck me," Nolan admitted. "I want to be between you two. Buried in her and impaled on your cock."

"That can be arranged." Jace smirked before coating his dick and replacing his fingers with the blunt head of it.

Laurel drew Nolan's attention, kissing him deeply. She trailed her fingers down the exposed column of his neck on the opposite side of his wound then over his pec as Jace advanced. The other man's cock was thick and long, spreading him open as if they'd done this a million times before. But they hadn't.

It was the first time he'd held Jace inside him, as he'd craved for so long. Being hugged tight by Laurel as Jace burrowed inside made him feel, finally, complete. At the center of their universe, surrounded by their love and attention and adoration, he believed them.

They loved him and hoped for the same things he did. A life together. One filled with lazy sex in the mornings, weekends watching Jace perform, filling a home of their own with the amazing art pieces Laurel crafted and took for granted. Peace when he wasn't in the middle of an underground war. Maybe someday even children of their own to raise as they wished they'd grown up.

Bliss would carry him through the darkest nights and cleanse the taint on his soul that threatened to stain him after spending too much time in the company of the dregs of humanity.

Nolan reached behind him, clasping Jace's flank and drawing him even closer, deeper. At the same time he leaned forward, sealing his mouth to Laurel's. She swallowed his moans and he did the same for her as the three of them fused into a single inseparable unit.

They stayed that way for a long time, barely moving, swaying together and enjoying simply being bonded so tightly. When the bliss of knowing he belonged to them heart and soul overwhelmed him, he poured himself into Laurel even as the pulses of his ass inspired Jace to flood him with his release.

Laurel cried out both of their names as she clenched then released in rolling waves that seemed to batter her for ages. It had been the best sex of his life and they'd hardly moved. But they were tangled together in a three-way embrace that he would never extract himself from.

With everything right in his world, and a wide smile on his face, Nolan closed his eyes. Jace and Laurel whispered to him together, "I love you."

"I love you too," he promised before drifting off in their arms, knowing they wouldn't let anything happen while he took a turn finally and truly resting.

22

Marcus collected another crystal glass from one of the roving waiters in tuxedos James had arranged for the grand opening of the Shields' new headquarters—which also served as a benign front for their less advertised, and much more expensive specialty security services—as well as their living spaces above it. They were normally jeans and T-shirt people, but James had insisted they clean up for his big night.

Kason and Jace had just finished a set on the temporary stage James had erected for them. Marcus had to admit, Jace was more talented than he'd realized, grabbing the focus of the entire room when he'd sung an original song he'd written for Nolan and Laurel while strumming a gorgeous sapphire guitar with mother of pearl inlay that gleamed in the LED lights.

Although their latest op hadn't gone exactly to plan, or maybe because of that, Marcus felt like celebrating. It could also be because he'd also moved into the apartment James had designed for him and the Powertools crew—

plus Mark—had helped bring to life. It had made him feel like the high roller he could be now if he chose. Modern, sleek, and fit for the wealthy, worldly operative he was now even if he still felt like the same middleclass Marcus he'd grown up as.

Sometimes he wondered how he'd gotten lucky enough to meet Jordan and become one of the team. His tendency to kick ass when necessary—a skill learned growing up as one of the few Black kids in his neighborhood—was an asset here, not something likely to get him thrown in the slammer like his mom had always warned.

Exciting job that paid incredibly well, did some good in the world even if no one ever knew he existed, a fat bank account, a plush place to live surrounded by like-minded and adventurous friends...well, he damn near had it all.

So why was he grimacing as he slammed his ridiculously priced and extremely smooth whiskey?

His stare landed on the most beautiful woman he'd ever laid eyes on. Dressed in a green satin gown with stiletto heels and glittery make-up, she drew his gaze even from across the command center conference room despite the people flitting between them.

He was used to seeing her in tactical gear or scrubs, which were hot enough on her. That dress with its plunging neckline and nonexistent back which put her toned body on display was about to inspire him to do something stupid.

Without conscious thought, he strolled in Kennedy's direction. A crowd gathered around the boardroom table, which had been wrapped in plastic and turned into a tattoo station for their resident artist, Blakely. It was becoming a ritual to hire her for their gatherings.

This time, it was Nolan in the hot seat.

A goofy grin plastered across his face, making him look more like a giant loveable puppy with action figure hair than the intimidating and lethal agent Marcus knew him to be in the field. Laurel perched on one side of him, holding his hand, while Jace stood behind him, his fingers resting on Nolan's shoulders. They stared at the spot where Blakely inked his lovers' names onto his arm.

Their relationship was solid. Permanent.

For the second time that evening, Marcus found himself jealous as hell. At least this time it was of flesh-and-blood humans instead of a satiny emerald dress that hugged Kennedy in all the right places. Damn, she was gorgeous.

Even better than that, she was brilliant, a doctor, and kept her head in an emergency. He'd witnessed her save more lives than he could count and never once flinch. He wouldn't ever say it out loud, but he'd been sure that he was watching Nolan's life drain away between his fingers that day they'd taken down Draven. That she'd saved him had taken his admiration to a whole new level.

Too bad she never bothered to give him so much as a bat of her long, thick lashes outside of their missions. Dr. Kennedy Emerson had zero interest in him, of that he was certain.

And now, on top of having to ignore her fine ass in tactical pants, he was also going to have to up his guard, because...fuck his life...as of a few hours ago, they were also neighbors. Damn James and his wicked sense of humor, putting their apartments side by side.

"Having fun, Marcus?" Speak of the little fucker. Their

command center manager strutted up to Marcus and slung an arm around his waist. He'd never seen the guy tipsy before and had to admit it was tough to stay grumpy at the cute bastard.

"Tons. Sorry about your car." Okay, he was being a bit of an ass, but shit talk carried them far in the Shields, and James was definitely one of them now.

"My car? What happened to it now?" James practically shrieked as he trotted toward the window.

"Don't worry. Bryce is having it towed to Hot Rods." Neil stepped up to his husband and shot Marcus a glare. "It'll be good as new again...soon."

"Who hurt my baby?" James shouted as he looked around the room.

"Oops." Nolan glanced up from staring at Laurel and Jace's names now permanently gracing his bulging biceps. "Sorry, bro. It's so small, I didn't see it when I backed in. I already told the Hot Rods I'd pay for the damage."

Chuckles surrounded them, though no one was brave enough to laugh outright with James fired up. He pouted, but Devon sandwiched him between her and Neil, then distracted him with a kiss. "Don't let it ruin your night. You've worked so hard. The office is perfect. Laurel, Jace, and Nolan moved in today so you'll have your sister nearby for good. Everyone loves it. You deserve to celebrate pulling off this huge project."

"Fine. But you better make sure she's good as new." James wagged his finger in Nolan's direction. The big guy saluted, then went back to admiring his new tat before dragging Laurel into his lap for a kiss that Jace leaned in and joined.

When Laurel pulled away, her face flushed, she said.

"There's something else I want to show you guys. All of you actually."

She looked up and met Ms. Brown and Tom's approving gazes before she drew a folded envelope from her purse.

"Is that...?" Jace's eyes bulged and Nolan's face threatened to split in half.

"An acceptance letter. Yeah, it is." Laurel was so pretty when the weight of her struggles vanished and only pure happiness remained. James flew to her along with Tom, Ms. Brown, Kate—who cuddled her tiny baby close to her chest—Sola, Kennedy, and all the rest of the people who adored her. At their core, Nolan and Jace wrapped her in one jumbo hug.

Those lucky bastards. Maybe if Marcus was willing to share Kennedy she would quit blowing him off. He'd seen the way she'd looked at Jordan, Kason, and Wren or James, Devon, and Neil. Sort of like she was staring at Jace, Laurel, and Nolan right then, that combination of wistful and sad making him ache to wrap her in his arms and promise her anything that would make her smile again.

While everyone else was distracted, Marcus swooped in, grabbing a glass off another tray for each of them before ushering Kennedy into a quiet corner behind the massive screens James had installed for them to view surveillance footage on. It surprised him when she didn't fight and instead accepted a drink from him, downing it in a few impressive glugs without so much as a cough.

"What's up?" he asked her, seeing straight through her painted-on smile. Despite the deep rose of her lips, it wasn't as beautiful as one of her natural and genuine sorts.

"Nothing." She shrugged, then eyed his glass too. "Just not always easy being solo among so many hopelessly in-love couples. Throuples. Whatever combo they've all got going on out there."

Marcus nodded. "I'm happy to partner up with you when we're not out in the field. We do make a hell of a team, you know?"

"I don't need some kind of pity date, thanks." She rolled her eyes.

Oh no. No way was he going to let her do that. Marcus advanced, backing her up against the wall hard enough that he heard a clunk as her shoulders and tight ass hit it. He planted his palm on the wall and leaned in. "Is that what you think I offered?"

He hoped she could tell how hard she'd made him in an instant. And if she had any lingering doubts, he was happy to chase them from her big, beautiful mind. God knew his own rational thoughts had fled because he dropped his face to hers and nibbled on her lip before sealing his mouth over hers.

She didn't shove him away or bite him and tell him to get his damn hands off her.

No, she kissed him back.

Kennedy's fingers traced the waves shaved into his hair as if she'd imagined doing it plenty of times before. She hiked one leg onto his hip and threw herself into eating at him as completely as she committed herself to saving lives on their missions.

Marcus let her take the lead for a little while, but it wasn't long before he met her lash for lash of her tongue. His free hand cupped her ass and dragged her close to his body as he leaned in. It was only when he had to breathe or pass out that he separated from her, his heart pounding against her chest as if he'd just finished his morning run.

"You have no idea how long I've been waiting for you to let me do that." Marcus slid his lips to her jaw then her neck as they caught their breath.

"It's a horrible idea." Kennedy started to stiffen in his grasp. Damn it, no.

"Because we work together?" Marcus wondered. "Jordan obviously doesn't give a damn. He practically gave Nolan a thumbs-up when he ordered him to shack up with Jace and Laurel."

"Not because our boss would care, but because being distracted in the field could get someone killed. And I have to wonder if Jordan might see that differently, given his past. I like what I do and I'm damn good at it. The last thing I need is for you, or anyone else, to fuck it up. I'm not sure I can work with someone I care about knowing they might be the next person I have to sew back together...if I'm even able to." Kennedy glanced away and swallowed hard. "Besides, I don't do dating. It's overrated."

Ah ha, *that* was closer to the truth. Or a more relevant reason anyway.

For one moment, he glimpsed the agony she tried so hard to hide most of the time.

"Who hurt you?" Marcus whispered.

"It doesn't matter because I learned my lesson and no one will ever do it again." Kennedy wiped her lips with the back of her hand, then slammed her eyes closed for a few seconds. When she opened them, every trace of heat and passion had vanished and only cold resolve remained. They transitioned from the cobalt of the wild ocean to the icy blue of frost in an instant. "Enjoy the party."

Marcus nodded and let her escape. For now.

The one thing Kennedy wasn't taking into account was the fact that he wasn't a damn quitter, and just like the times they spent weeks staking out the location for an op, he could be patient when needed.

After all, now they weren't only co-workers. They were also neighbors. Avoiding the attraction between them was going to be impossible. Sooner or later, they were going to have to tackle it head on, and he would be ready when that day came.

Marcus held his glass up in her direction, then drained it in one long sip.

When her gaze latched on the flex of his throat and the wetness lingering on his lips from the amber liquid, he grinned. Whenever it happened, and they finally caved to the sparks that always flew when they were together, it was going to be worth the wait.

~

To FIND out who might bring Marcus and Kennedy together, read their story LOST.

If you'd like to start at the very beginning with the Powertools Crew, you can download a discounted boxset of the first six books HERE.

Yes, I know it says complete series but I wrote a seventh book more recently and haven't gotten around to updating the boxset yet, sorry!

You can find the seventh Powertools book, More the Merrier, HERE.

They are also featured in four books in the Powertools: The Original Crew Returns series starting with Screwed HERE

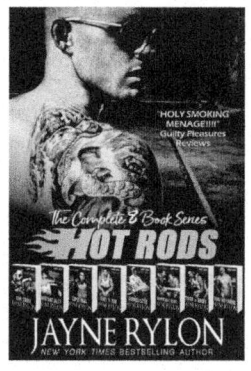

If you missed out on the Powertools: Hot Rods series, you can buy all eight books in a discounted single-volume boxset by clicking HERE.

To read more about the Hot Rides gang, start with Quinn, Trevon, and Devra's story, Wild Ride, click HERE.

Did you know Jayne brought the original Powertools crew back for four more books? Click HERE to get caught up.

CLAIM A $5 GIFT CERTIFICATE

Jayne is so sure you will love her books, she'd like you to try any one of your choosing for free. Claim your $5 gift certificate by signing up for her newsletter. You'll also learn about freebies, new releases, extras, appearances, and more!

www.jaynerylon.com/newsletter

WHAT WAS YOUR FAVORITE PART?

Did you enjoy this book? If so, please leave a review and tell your friends about it. Word of mouth and online reviews are immensely helpful and greatly appreciated.

JAYNE'S SHOP

Check out Jayne's online shop for autographed print books, direct download ebooks, reading-themed apparel up to size 5XL, mugs, tote bags, notebooks, Mr. Rylon's wood (you'll have to see it for yourself!) and more.
www.jaynerylon.com/shop

LISTEN UP!

The majority of Jayne's books are also available in audio format on Audible, Amazon and iTunes.

ABOUT THE AUTHOR

 Jayne Rylon is a *New York Times* and *USA Today* bestselling author who has sold more than one million books. She has received numerous industry awards including the Romantic Times Reviewers' Choice Award for Best Indie Erotic Romance and the Swirl Award, which recognizes excellence in diverse romance. She is an Honor Roll member of the Romance Writers of America. Her stories used to begin as daydreams in seemingly endless business meetings, but now she is a full time author, who employs the skills she learned from her straight-laced corporate existence in the business of writing. She lives in Ohio with her husband, the infamous Mr. Rylon, and their cat, Frodo. When she can escape her purple office, she loves to travel the world, avoid speeding tickets in her beloved Sky, SCUBA dive, hunt Pokemon, and–of course–read.

Jayne Loves To Hear From Readers
www.jaynerylon.com
contact@jaynerylon.com
PO Box 10, Pickerington, OH 43147

facebook.com/jaynerylon

twitter.com/JayneRylon

instagram.com/jaynerylon

youtube.com/jaynerylonbooks

bookbub.com/profile/jayne-rylon

amazon.com/author/jaynerylon

ALSO BY JAYNE RYLON

4-EVER

A New Adult Reverse Harem Series

4-Ever Theirs

4-Ever Mine

EVER AFTER DUET

Reverse Harem Featuring Characters From The 4-Ever Series

Fourplay

Fourkeeps

EVER & ALWAYS DUET

Reverse Harem Featuring Characters from the 4-Ever and Ever After Duets

Four Money

Four Love

POWERTOOLS: THE ORIGINAL CREW

Five Guys Who Get It On With Each Other & One Girl. Enough Said?

Kate's Crew

Morgan's Surprise

Kayla's Gift

Devon's Pair

Nailed to the Wall

Hammer it Home

More the Merrier *NEW*

POWERTOOLS: HOT RODS

Powertools Spin Off. Keep up with the Crew plus...

Seven Guys & One Girl. Enough Said?

King Cobra

Mustang Sally

Super Nova

Rebel on the Run

Swinger Style

Barracuda's Heart

Touch of Amber

Long Time Coming

POWERTOOLS: HOT RIDES

Powertools and Hot Rods Spin Off.

Menage and Motorcycles

Wild Ride

Slow Ride

Hard Ride

Joy Ride

Rough Ride

POWERTOOLS: RETURN OF THE CREW

The original crew is back with more steamy menage stories!

Screwed

Drilled

Grind

Pound

MEN IN BLUE

Hot Cops Save Women In Danger

Night is Darkest

Razor's Edge

Mistress's Master

Spread Your Wings

Wounded Hearts

Bound For You

DIVEMASTERS

Sexy SCUBA Instructors By Day, Doms On A Mega-Yacht By Night

Going Down

Going Deep

Going Hard

STANDALONE

Menage

Middleman

Nice & Naughty

Contemporary

Where There's Smoke

Report For Booty

COMPASS BROTHERS

Modern Western Family Drama Plus Lots Of Steamy Sex

Northern Exposure

Southern Comfort

Eastern Ambitions

Western Ties

COMPASS GIRLS

Daughters Of The Compass Brothers Drive Their Dads Crazy And Fall In Love

Winter's Thaw

Hope Springs

Summer Fling

Falling Softly

COMPASS BOYS

Sons Of The Compass Brothers Fall In Love

Heaven on Earth

Into the Fire

Still Waters

Light as Air

PLAY DOCTOR

Naughty Sexual Psychology Experiments Anyone?

Dream Machine

Healing Touch

RED LIGHT

A Hooker Who Loves Her Job

Complete Red Light Series Boxset

FREE - Through My Window - FREE

Star

Can't Buy Love

Free For All

PICK YOUR PLEASURES

Choose Your Own Adventure Romances!

Pick Your Pleasure

Pick Your Pleasure 2

RACING FOR LOVE

MMF Menages With Race-Car Driver Heroes

Complete Series Boxset

Driven

Shifting Gears

PARANORMALS

Vampires, Witches, And A Man Trapped In A Painting

Paranormal Double Pack Boxset

Picture Perfect

Reborn

PENTHOUSE PLEASURES

Naughty Manhattanite Neighbors Find Kinky Love

Taboo

Kinky

Sinner

Mentor

ROAMING WITH THE RYLONS

Non-fiction Travelogues about Jayne & Mr. Rylon's Adventures

Australia and New Zealand

Made in the USA
Monee, IL
12 June 2021